Fire Kissed

L.C. SON

Contents

Copyright

www.LCSonBooks.com

Paperback ISBN 979-8-9862237-2-8
Hardcover ISBN 979-8-9862237-3-5

Edited by The Fiction Fix
Paperback Cover Design by Covers in Color
Hardcover Design by L.C. Son
Interior Formatting by Megan Parker
Art Illustration by Gigi's Lab

About Fire Kissed

Villains aren't meant to be loved, especially ones who betray all you hold dear.

How can the villain of her world be the hero of her heart?

Tired of towing the line and being in the shadow of her larger-than-life twin and the cousin she admires, Rae Vereen is finally going after what she wants. What she wants just so happens to be a Son of the Netherworld and the enemy of her family. Is Rae willing to pay the price if what she wants goes against the family she loves?

A Note from L.C. Son

My sincere thanks to you for choosing *Fire Kissed,* book one in the Fire Duet. Truly, there is no better reward for an author than to release the inner musings of my creative mind into the world. None of this would be possible without readers like you.

For some of you, this is your introduction to my books, while for others, you're ready to plunge right into reading. Either way, I'd like to set your expectations.

While this book is a standalone it may be helpful to know that the book takes place right after the events of *One Winter's Kiss.* There will be some reference to the events of *One Winter's Kiss* in this book, but can still be read separately. One Winter's Kiss has a more fairytale-like setting that is built on insta-love and forbidden romance. Fire Kissed, and the Fire Duet as a whole, however, builds on the forbidden romance trope in a darker fantasy setting than that of its predecessor. Please keep reading for a complete content warning.

Additionally, it is important to note the characters in this book often speak in a more regal fashion although they are set in a modern world. In this book, hierarchy is real and titles such as Lord and Lady are used both respectively and affectionately. Plainly put, the characters really operate in their buble in the modern world–and beyond–and it seems to work for them.

Hopefully, you'll catch their cadence and flow with the storyline without troubling yourself with semantics.

Again, thank you for your readership and happy reading!

Dream Well,
LC

Content Warning

This book is intended for mature readers, aged 18+. The content of this book may contain material not suitable for all readers and/or those with sensitivities to the topics of death, grief, violence against supernatural characters, pillow talk, and steamy situations.

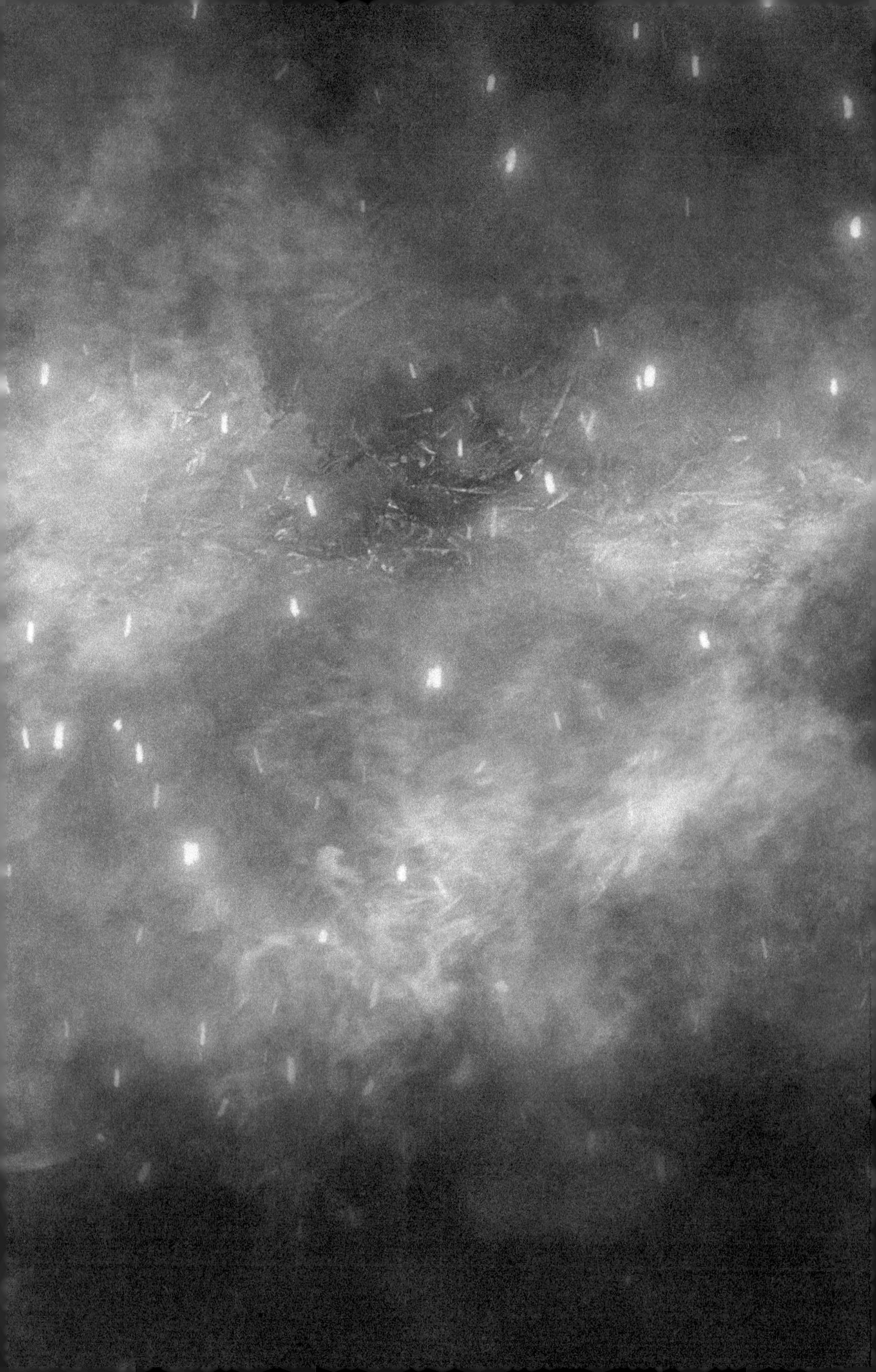

Prologue

RAE

The Beginning of Us

LIGHT FLASHED BRIGHTLY past my eyes, nearly blinding me. I wasn't prepared for the camera to snap a shot of Kharon and me. Sure, it's a sight I'd love to have as a keepsake, but I'm hardly photogenic, especially today.

"Are you cold?" Kharon asks, wrapping his black trench coat around me as we dangle over the icy snow.

I knew it was a bad idea to go skiing with Ross today. My twin had no intention of hitting the slopes at all. His only reason for coming was to see if he could get close to that new lumberjack staying at the ski lodge. Ross met him, all right, and ditched me the first chance he got.

So, what did I do? Continue with our plans to ski, like an idiot. Unfortunately for me, I got scared. No sooner had I made it to the hilltop did I quickly find my way back to the bunny slopes where a novice like me belongs.

I am an okay skier at best, nowhere as skillful as my brother, but I trudged my way onward, as if I had nothing to fear.

Thankfully, fate knew better.

I have no business on a black diamond run, not at all. I suppose that's why my feet are now suspended over the snow as my fear of heights gnaws at me, inwardly scolding myself for such a foolhardy attempt.

If I weren't stuck on this lift with Kharon, I might be deserving of my lot for attempting something I knew was stupid. Still, maybe I didn't grab the short straw like I normally do.

After only being stuck for a few seconds, Kharon quickly offered his trench as a shield from the wind while simultaneously wrapping his arms around me. His warmth reminds me of a bright sunny day, despite the freezing winds whipping around us.

Looking up at his grayish-blue eyes, I can't help wanting to drown myself in the entirety of him.

"Rae?" he questions, breaking me from my lingering gaze on the delicate stubble along his jaw and the enchanting way his dirty blonde hair blows in the wind, framing his ruggedly handsome face perfectly.

"Yes?" I chattered as the wind hits my face.

"You're freezing!" he exclaims, pulling me deeper into his embrace. "Come on, get under here. We've got to keep you warm." Pressing himself against me, I shiver when he slides his arm around my waist, slightly grazing my breast. Though it wasn't intentional, Kharon's eyes lock with mine almost apologetically, but I bury my head into his chest, hopeful he doesn't pull away. "Is this better?"

Damn, even the tremble in his nervous voice is sexy as hell.

My heart races, wishing he'd *touch* me again. "Much better," I whisper, inhaling his sweet, smokey cigar scent. Secondhand smoke never smelled so good.

"Well, I guess neither of us thought we'd find ourselves caught on this contraption when we woke up this morning," Kharon says with a small chuckle.

"Nope." I release a soft giggle. "Didn't quite make my to-do list." His scent is so intoxicating, I can't help but take in large gulps of his aroma. Another wind whips by us and he strengthens his hold on me, pulling me closer. Swinging my leg over his lap, I snuggled myself deeper into his embrace, enjoying the steady strumming of his heart under my ear. My hand touches the soft cotton of his sweater vest, and I'm impressed I can still feel the outline of his muscular form beneath it all.

Smiling at me as his eyes search my face, he asks, "So, Rae, are you a daredevil of sorts?"

"Me? No!" I shriek, looking away from him. "What makes you think that?"

Gazing down under his coat at me, he moves a few stray curls from my face, brandishing a smile that warms parts of me that have never been touched. "Well, this is a black diamond run. You've got to be pretty good to take this one on."

"Oh, yeah, that." I frown, thinking of how silly I must look.

"Not that it's a bad thing, Rae," Kharon soothes, lifting my chin back up to meet his gaze. "It's okay to want to try something new, even if you have to go at it alone."

Hunching my shoulders, I press my head back into his chest. I like the way he smells, and the cadence of his heartbeat is soothing.

"What about you?" I ask, keeping my face planted deep into his chest. "Are you a thrill junkie or something?"

Kharon laughs, squeezing me as he does, grunting softly as his hand once more sweeps the side of my breast.

I don't think that one was as unintentional as the first, and I can't say I mind.

"Or something," he murmurs into my hair. "Um—I mean, I had some business to tend to on the other side of the hill with Don Addy," he says, pulling back a bit. Shifting himself, my leg grazes his crotch, and I feel the hardness he was clearly trying to hide.

Our eyes connect, and I let my hand trail along his chest as his stare warms my body. I know he's got me by almost two decades. I also know he can have any woman on the island, but in this moment, with the way his eyes lock with mine, I'm the only woman in the world.

Sure, he may only see the nineteen-year-old niece of his closest friend and business associate when he looks at me, but right now, I can only hope he sees so much more.

"Oh, that's right. Next to Uncle El, you're the big businessman on this icicle." I chuckle against his chest as I think about how he's quite the talk of our little Nova Scotian town. Arriving here a few years ago, Mr. Kharon Nyx has made quite an impression on the locals. While my uncle is still held in the highest regard, the mystique of Kharon is hard to ignore.

He laughs, and his sweet smoky scent tickles my nose again. "Well, I don't know about all that. I'm just a lowly ferryman at heart. What about you, Rae?"

At his inquiry, I feel nervousness bubble in the pit of my stomach. The subject of *me* makes me uncomfortable.

"What about me?" I ask, trying to push myself up and out of his hold. Unfortunately for me, he tightens his arms, locking me in place.

"Oh no you don't," Kharon grumbles, his tone more authoritative than before. Gazing up at him as he cradles me in his arms, I find comfort in the small smile forming at the corners of his mouth. Forcing a faux chortle, he lets his smile spread across his face. "It's my job to keep you warm, little one." He tightens his grasp around me, and I know his possessive tone should scare me, but it's just the opposite. "Since you're my little prisoner while we're trapped on this ski lift, you might as well tell me a little about yourself. All I know is that you're Elysian's niece."

Fidgeting with my curls laying against my ear, I feel my nerves ease a bit. I don't know if it's the comfort I feel in his arms or what, but I could stay here forever.

Even more, this is the first time someone has asked me about me. Sure, Ross and Win know me, but beyond them, most people don't pay much attention to the awkward, freckled twin of my more outspoken brother, or even see me beyond the shadow of my stunning cousin, who pretty much oversees every facet of the family business. To most, I'm just the lowly girl in the background.

"There's not much to tell," I whisper, twirling my hair between my fingers.

Grabbing my hand, Kharon stills my twitching. "I highly doubt that, Rae. I think there's more hidden behind your eyes than most could imagine. I'd like to know about the Rae no one else sees."

Sure, I'd love to tell him about my dream to open my own bakery one day, but I hardly have time to process Kharon's sentiment when another strong wind whips our carriage, rocking us back and forth. The motion startles me, but Kharon is unmoved as he braces me in his arms. If the freezing temperature wasn't enough to remind me I was indeed awake, I'd swear I was dreaming.

This is the moment I never thought would come. When Kharon jumped in the ski lift with me earlier, I thought this would be a quiet zip trip over the hill. Normally, I only see him when he's with my uncle. Never did I think I'd have a moment alone with Kharon Nyx, but here we are.

He slides his palm over my cheek, his thumb slowly outlining the curves of my mouth. "Rae," Kharon breathes my name, and the nutty scent of a smoky maple cigar explodes across my senses, drawing me in.

"Yes," I moan, desperate for his kiss. *Yes, his kiss*. The one man who alone is the lover of my dreams. The one man whose hands I imagine are my own when I'm alone at night. The elusive bachelor. The one I've hoped has remained so because he was waiting for me. Well, here I am, of age and ready.

"Rae!" I hear my name called once more, but this time, it's different. "Rae, are you okay up there?" Jolted from my thoughts, I look down to see Ross with Mr. Addy. "Don't worry," he screams at us. "They'll have this rig moving in no time."

Slowly scooting himself away from me, an awkward smile frames Kharon's face as he presses the would-be wrinkles out of his pants. "Well, I guess I can no longer keep you hostage," Kharon smiles nervously.

"Too bad," I grumble, tossing my hair away from my face. "I was starting to like being your hostage."

Kharon's gaze darkens as he tightens his smile, and I swear I see a tent forming at his crotch. I think he liked me being his hostage, too.

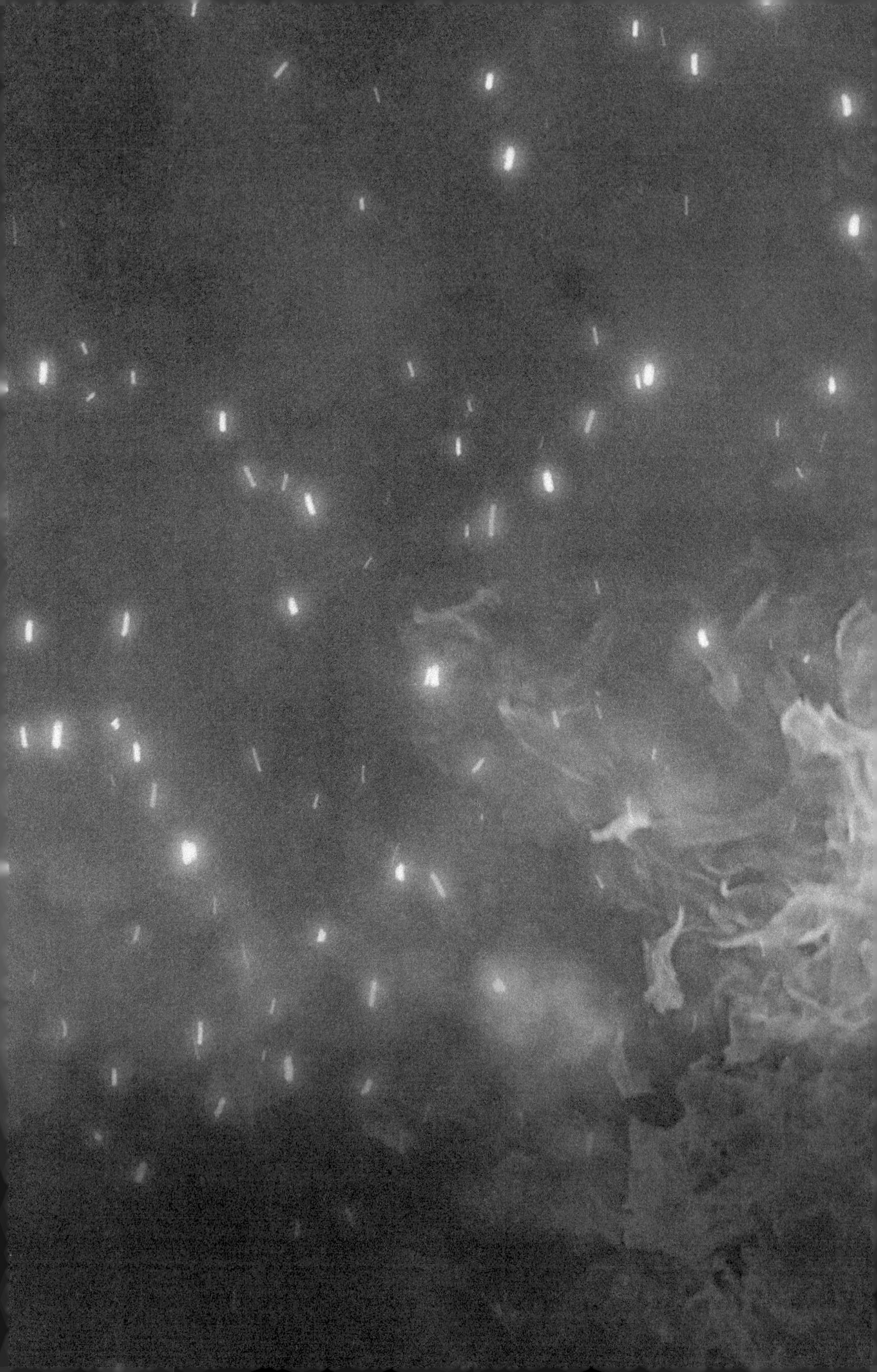

KHARON

The Beginning of Us

As thankful as I am to not have Rae freezing on the ski lift, releasing her hurts me more than she'll ever understand.

Although it was our first time alone together, today wasn't the first time I noticed her. Since the day I met Elysian's family, it's only been Rae Vereen who holds my attention. Her brother, Ross, is a ham, hogging most of the spotlight for himself, while Elysian does all he can to push his precious daughter, Winter, to the forefront. Still, it's Rae whose beauty makes my hollowed heart leap.

That's why I ended my meeting with Don Addy abruptly: I

spotted Rae making her way down the hillside, alone. For the first time, she wasn't surrounded by her family or her friends. I knew it was the only chance I'd have to be alone with her.

Sure, a twinge of lust led me to barge past everyone in line to get a seat next to her on the ski lift, but it was my need to undue this wretched curse that forced me to freeze the lift long enough to come away with a strand of her hair. Thankfully, I was able to swipe a small curl without her even wincing. Hopefully, this will be enough to test the magic of the obol, to finally release her cousin Melchior from the bondage of the Changelings' dark power.

Only a kiss of love by one bound by blood to Melchior will free him from his imprisonment. I waited as long as I could after she became of age to make my move, but I've been fearful to try.

For a while, I'd suspected the affection I felt for Rae was shared. Today only confirmed my suspicions.

Now, if only she could *love* a wretch like me. Only Rae's love can free her cousin from bondage and bring a finality to this cursed life of mine. I only want to be free, not a bound ferryman destined for the darkness of the fires of the Underworld.

Once Rae and I made it back to the carriage station, I flung my coat off her, quickly got out of the ski lift, and rushed past the mob of folks waiting to see if we were okay. Allowing myself one last look at us on the camera replay monitor, the sight of us together warms my dark soul.

Still, I don't linger.

Most of my abruptness was because I needed to hide the enormous effect Rae had on my manhood. Although I'm sure she felt me beneath her leg, there was no need to bring undue attention. The last thing I'd want is for others to think less of her. The locals are more likely to judge Rae than me, so if I had to look like the businessman who had more important things to do than calm a frightened woman, so be it.

I only hope my sudden departure doesn't sully the moment we

shared today. Once I know for sure that she can bring Melchior out of his doomed state, my next and only goal is to make Rae mine.

Flinging my coat to the floor the moment I arrive home, I rush to Melchior's prism, clutching Rae's hair and brandishing the obol from around my neck, hopeful to beckon the Changelings to my hovel. It brings me no joy to be caught in their dark web of witchery, but alas, here I stand.

Slowly, their dark, hazy mist clouds my view, funneling around me like a thick blanket. "*Whilst you call and now awake, bound to Sheol, seal thy fate. Longing heart, with lust you fill, the mate you wish, denies you still. No ray of light, summer nor spring, only in winter will fortune ring.*"

Dark figures with callous grins shriek their sound, echoing throughout the cave. As I stare at their ominous faces, the merriment once raging in my heart plummets to the ground.

While their haunting sonnet is muddled in the language of men, being of the Netherworld, I know the meaning too well.

Rae isn't the one.

Winter is.

But I don't want Winter. I want Rae.

The power of the obol still holds the Young Lord Elysian under the Changelings' enchantment. Though his eyes can barely be seen through a mortal lens, I spy his sad eyes watching me through his prison. For years, I promised Melchior I'd save him. I don't know if he understands anything I'm saying behind the thick chasm holding him hostage, but I can only hope he knows I'm doing everything in my power to free him.

The thick mist of the Changelings thins, and anger plows through me. I refuse to let them leave me like this!

"There has to be another way!" I shout.

Letting out a sharp, shrieking howl, their darkness hurls around me once more. "This, Son of Erebus, is the only way. Only the blood of an Elysian can unbind the young lord's tether to your fate. The one to whom this strand belongs is not of Elysian blood!"

Damn! Rae must only be Elysian's niece by marriage, not blood. How did I not know this?

The Changelings leave me little time to ponder their words before striking me with a harsh gale, pinning me tight against the cold slab of Melchior's prison.

With hissing sounds whirling around the darkened cave, a small, shrill chortle burrows its way through the phantom's mist. *"To the obol remain bound, lest to love thine heart be found. Only the truest kiss will set him free or in time to come in Sheol he shall be!"*

No sooner do their riddled musings ring in my ears, am I released from their tight grip, straining for air on the cold floor.

My body contorts as a shooting ache rips through me, and I cry out in pain. "Fu—argh!"

"Brother!" I hear my sister, Moirai, call to me, her voice bouncing off the onyx stone in the center of the room. "Kharon, please!" She pleads louder as a white light shoots out from the darkened corner.

"Go away, Moirai!" I shout back, writhing in pain on the floor.

"Is it happening again?" Moirai asks, her voice consoling me from afar.

This isn't the first time my sister has seen this happen. Every time the Changelings want to *teach me a lesson*, they speed up my aging. In mortal time, I shouldn't look any older than Melchior, maybe in my mid-twenties. Instead, I look like someone who's made more than forty rotations around the sun. Sure, the Sons of Erebus, the ferrymen, are known as aged men charting the River Styx of the Netherworld, but in the lifespan of the Netherworld, I have a millennium to go before I even begin to age. I suppose, if there was any benefit to being a child of the Netherworld, it would be that without the sun's influence, we age far slower than mortals.

"Yes," I choke out, slowly forcing myself to stand. Stumbling toward the onyx stone, I lean against the cave wall and gaze into the stone. Though my body is still aching, it does me good just to see the murky reflection of my sister smiling back at me.

"Well, it doesn't look as bad as the last time. You're just a little grayer at your hairline. You're perfect all the same." Moirai always finds a way to make me smile. Even though my sister is just as much a prisoner as I am, she chooses to see the good in this life. I love that about her.

Still, being the eldest, it's also my job to look after her. "I'm sorry, dear sister. I promise, I'll get you out of there. I'll get us both out from under their control!" I snap, pounding my fist hard against the wall.

"Kharon, please! This is not your doing! Our father sold us to this lot well before we had a choice. Just as I sit as a Fate at their leisure, so do you chart the seas at their behest. All is not lost, dear brother. As I said before, this was the only way to free us." Moirai's voice is calming, like water trickling over rocks. Even though I have less faith than my sister in the path we've chosen, listening to her always tempers my rage. "Besides, I've never seen you this happy."

Stepping back from the wall, I squint, working hard to make out her face through the dark stone. "What? I am anything but happy right now, sister. I think the mist clouds your vision." I laugh.

"I'm not speaking of now," she begins as the stone brightens. I finally see her face in full, and she gives me a knowing look. "The expectancy and glee in your steps as you rushed in here, holding that strand in your hand -- would this be from the woman you mentioned?"

Opening my palm, I notice I'm still holding the curly strand of Rae's hair. Nodding, sadness creeps over me again as I recall the changelings' words. "She is not the one," I mumble, leaning my head on my forearm against the cold wall.

"Do you trust me, brother?" Moirai's tone is quick, snapping me out of my sulking state. Mouthing *yes* in reply, I nod once more, unsure what new challenge my sister has in mind. "Then do as the Wretched Ones demand. Pursue Winter Elysian, for it is only in your pursuit that you will find our freedom. The Fates have decreed it so."

Despite my misgivings, I know one thing is true. I cannot outrun fate.

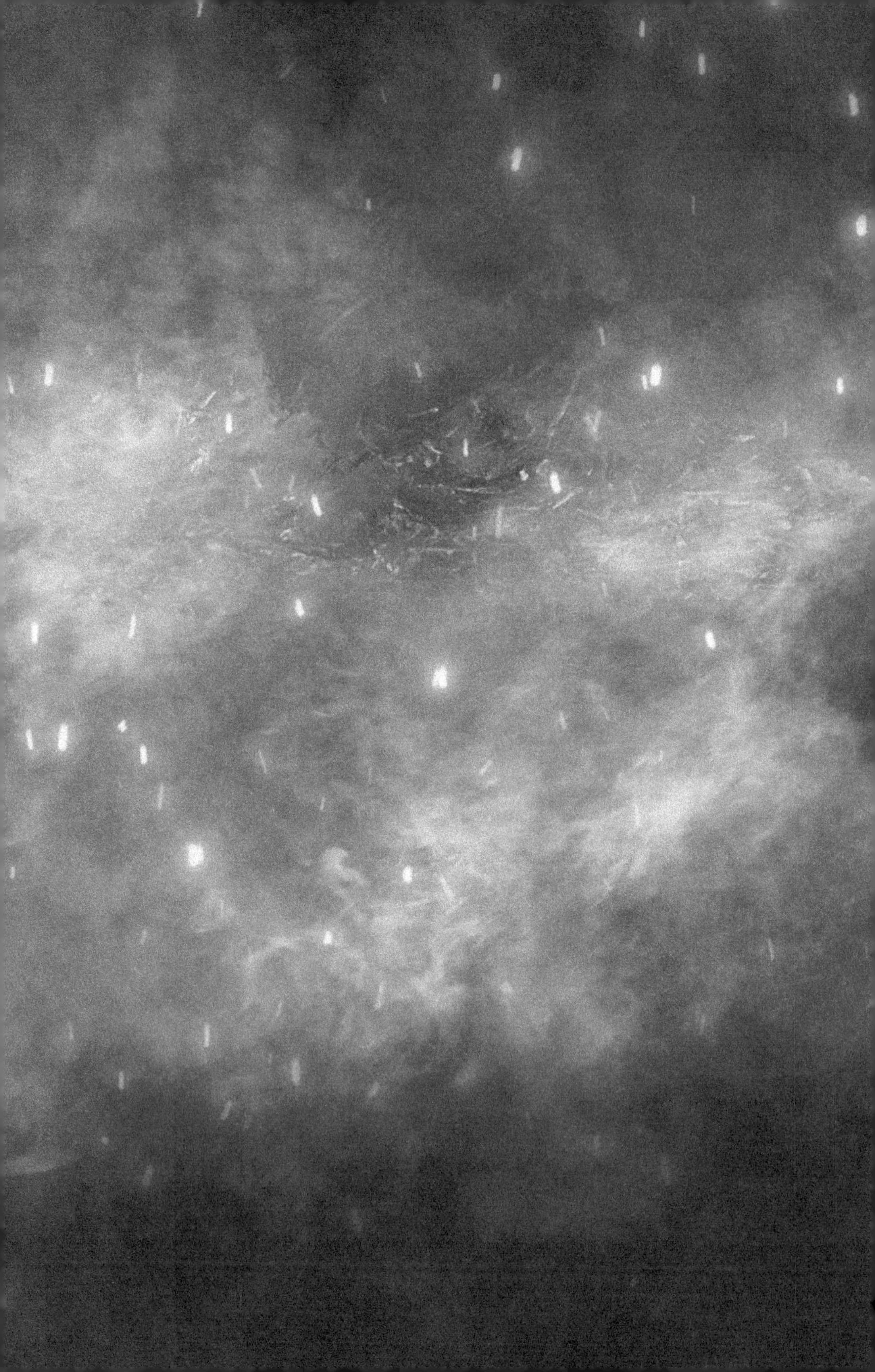

One

RAE

Three Years Later

It's Christmas Eve, and where do I find myself? Not nestled in front of a roaring fire, sipping my favorite chamomile tea, listening to my aunt play Christmas songs on her baby grand piano while Ross enlists me to wrap his last-minute gifts. No, I'm not that fortunate.

Instead, I'm here, trudging through a snowy forest, seeking out a man who has kept my heart in a cage while I fawned after his every step. I watched like an idiot, my heart banging on its iron-clad bars, as he made every attempt to be with my cousin Winter.

Yet, here I am. Hiding behind the tree line, I try to stay quiet as I watch the Guard search Kharon's shipyard, looking for him. While most of the Guard moves with wolfen and vampiric speed, the strength of my heart alone allows me to keep up with them, albeit at a ridiculously slow mortal pace.

I don't think I've ever been to this side of the island. As a matter of fact, I don't think I knew it even existed. This side of the island feels different, darker somehow. It's not the picturesque, almost fairytale-like island where I grew up at Elysian Manor. The air even feels muggy and dank, not like the crisp wintry air near my home. I should be scared. I *am* scared, but that doesn't stop me from following them around like an idiot.

An idiot who just learned that not only did Kharon keep my cousin Melchior prisoner all these long years but witnessed how hurt he was when he saw Winter kiss Lux, freeing Melchior from his prison. A part of me wonders if it caused him pain because he really loves her, or if it was all part of some grand scheme.

Either way, I need to know.

It's bad enough that since our moment in the ski lift, I've somehow tethered my heart to his. No, to add insult to injury, I'm apparently a glutton for punishment. I want him to look me in the eyes and tell me I've been a doting fool all these years.

Reason would be well to suggest I'm a fool, if it weren't for him ripping me from the clutches of Don Addy's son, Kevin, on the dance floor at the summer solstice festival. Or perhaps it was the time the local mechanic got too handsy with me, was mysteriously injured the next day and has since walked on the other side of the road when Kharon was near.

I am no fool.

Maybe I am.

Either way, it ends tonight or begins as something new.

"He's not here!" a man shouts to another, who I knew was named Dranoel, from the docking post.

Dranoel looks around, sniffing a few more times before quickly shouting more orders. I can only hope my scent is undetectable. I should have doused myself with red mud before following the Guard's search for Kharon. Uncle El always said it keeps the foxes and coyotes away. The lumber guys swear by it, chalking their boots with the clay before heading into the woods. Too bad I didn't have time to test the theory.

Luckily, the Guard is more concerned about finding Kharon than looking for me.

"Head back to the manor!" Dranoel waves his arm to the Guard and the men begin making their way back up the hill.

Crouched low, I peer through the tree line and I notice a few branches shaking, but I don't see anyone. Narrowing my gaze, I look around, wondering if it was some nocturnal creature nearby. My nerves get the best of me as I watch the Guard move farther from my sight. I know better to be in the woods this late at night on my own. My mind keeps replaying the story of Ross and Win's encounter with the bear in the woods, and a twinge of fear sweeps through me. Here I am, putting my very life on the line for a man who clearly isn't interested in me. For what?

I hear another sound brush through the leaves, and I turn around to see reflective eyes staring back at me, a low snarl in its throat.

A coyote.

Backing up, I inwardly berate myself for coming out here. I know better. What was I thinking?

Another snarl snakes through the trees, and another pair of reflective eyes glow back at me as they cry in a harmonious wail. Looking over my shoulder, I don't see the Guard anymore. Crap! I could have yelled to the Guard for help, but they're long gone now.

Slowly, the tawny gray coyotes stray out from under the bushes and closer to me, snarling and baring their canines. Craning their heads upward, their short tails stiffen and my heart pounds heavy in my chest.

I shouldn't be here. I suppose I'll get what I deserve. What's worse, I am alone. I left my family.

While they're likely all too enthralled with the engagement of my cousin Win and Lux to notice my absence, I know it won't be long before Ross wonders where I've gone.

Or at least I hope so.

I take a step back, hopeful I'll make it to the clearing and toward the shoreline before the animals can get to me. I ditched my heels back at the manor, so all I have to contend with is this wretched gown and the cold, since I forgot my coat. The lack of a bustled train may prove to my downfall, though, as I fall back when my train gets caught on a thick tree branch.

The two coyotes rear back, ready to pounce, when their eyes hover over my shoulder. As they do, I'm too fearful to look behind me, and I keep my eyes trained on the two menacing creatures in front of me. When a faint sweet and smoky scent wafts past my nose, though, my trepidation settles.

Still, I don't have time to revel in it for long when I'm lifted from the ground from behind. I part my lips to scream, but my mouth is quickly covered by a gloved hand. Squirming, I try to wiggle from my captor's grip, but my attempts are futile. Before I have a moment to understand what's happening, everything goes silent as I'm carted inside a dark cave.

Tossed aside onto a strangely pillowy mound of satiny fabrics, I jump up, looking around the cavern, wondering who brought me here. Turning around, I'm shocked when a candle brightens my view, revealing Kharon standing before me.

Two

KHARON

HERS IS the face I only want to see -- *need to see* -- but not like this.

I can't stand for her to see me looking like a disheveled old man, a shell of the man I once was, the man she deserves. With Lux not only holding my obol, but also freeing Melchior with Winter's kiss, I am fully susceptible to the ferryman's curse.

Why I chose to listen to Moirai and take the Changelings up on their deal is beyond me. I knew better, and I know better still. I've long known of Changeling treachery. Anything they offer has a price. For our freedom, I thought I could do what was necessary.

I failed.

Now, my sister is left to suffer through their dark witchery, forever hostage as a Fate. No doubt they intend to use Moirai's premonitions to overthrow the kingdoms of the Netherworld and ultimately find a way back into the mortal world.

To my chagrin, I also failed Rae.

With the way she looks at me now, not only does she likely see the frame of the decrepit fool who kept her cousin hostage all these years, she has no idea I am just as much a prisoner as Melchior ever was.

Rae has no idea how much I craved to be the man she deserved. Clearly, whatever aspirations I had are now for naught.

"Kharon?" Rae murmurs, tilting her head away from the direct light of the candle. Her eyes stalk up and down my body, and I can only imagine how much I must repulse her.

"Why are you here?" I snap, turning away. My tone is harsher than I intended, but I can't stand her seeing me like this. An aching pain shoots through me, and I know my demise is near. Making my way to the corner, I set the candle on the ledge, surprised when I turn to find her on my heel.

"You brought me here," she whispers back, looking around the cave, hugging herself. I notice the short sleeves of her gown and realize she's cold. Though a part of me is upset she's out in the cold dressed as she is, it doesn't stop me from wanting to keep her warm.

I shuck my trench coat off as quick as my aching, aging body will allow, tossing it around her shoulders. A small smile frames her face, but I take note at how she briefly inhales the collar of my coat. That small, doting motion sends fire straight to my manhood, but I dismiss the notion as quickly as it comes. I'm sure her only thoughts are of who I once was, not the thing I am now.

"Only to keep you from becoming a coyote feast," I grumble, lighting another candle.

Ripping my coat from her shoulders, Rae folds it in half and throws it at me. It hits the candle, catching flame. If her eyes were daggers, I'd be dead. Still, it would be better to die by her hand than this curse.

"I'd rather be a nocturnal feast!" Rae bites back, marching toward the entrance.

Quickly stomping out the small fire on my coat, I move in front of her, preventing her exit.

"Get out of my way, Kharon!" Rae's eyes lock with mine, and the glassy puddles of tears she's barely holding back make my heart melt.

I want to reach out to touch her, comfort her, but I know better. The way Rae looks at me tells me she's wary of me. She has every reason to be. "I'm sorry, Rae. I didn't mean it the way it came out."

With another daggered stare, Rae leans away, appalled at the sight of me. "Really, Kharon? That's all you have to say for yourself? I come out here, risk my life to see if you're okay, and all you have to say is that isn't how you wanted it to come out? Wow! I'm a bigger idiot than I thought—"

"Hold on," I say, side stepping her view of the exit. "You came out here to see if *I'm okay?*"

Rae's posture softens, but she still maintains her distance. "Yes, of course." Her soft reply matches the genuine care I suddenly see in her eyes.

As much as I should be comforted by her reply, Rae's words confuse me. "Why? After everything—"

"You know why, Kharon." Rae's tender eyes search mine, but still, she doesn't move.

Casting my gaze toward the ground, I work hard to avert my eyes from her tight-locked stare. I don't want her looking at the wretched thing I've become. With wilted, mole-ridden skin, a hooked nose, and hunched posture, I resemble a monster best befitting a bell tower, rather than the presence of one so lovely.

Seeing my reflection in a small puddle at my feet, I thrash my boot through the water and turn away from her. *I'm hideous!*

This time, it's Rae stopping me from walking away from her.

"Oh no you don't!" she snaps, grabbing my shoulder. "You're *my hostage* now, Kharon! You're going to listen to what I have to say."

Rae tightens her small hands, squeezing my shoulder stronger than I would have thought her capable. Being in her hold feels good. *Too good.* Looking at her perfect, honey-hued face isn't helping matters. I want nothing more than to bring her in my arms, but I can't. As far as she knows, I'm the villain of the story.

"It's not safe for you here, Rae. You should leave." This time, my curt tone is intentional. I don't know whether the Changelings will return, or if they're done with me entirely. All evidence suggests the latter, as my rapid aging tells me they've left me to die here. That's what I plan to do. Die here. Alone.

Rae has suffered enough pain today. I do not wish for her to endure anymore. Although, with the way she's looking at me now, she might enjoy a front seat to my demise.

Squaring her shoulders and lifting her chin, she smirks. "No." Rae's resolute tone is quick, almost biting. "I see what you're trying to do, Kharon Nyx. *I see you.*" Slowly, her gaze drags along my face and through the entirety of me, smiling sweetly as she does. I don't know what she sees in a monster like me, but with one foot at death's door, it costs me nothing to leave the door open.

Three

RAE

Kharon's darkened stare lingers on me, and I wish I knew what he was thinking.

Do I look like a fool? Maybe I look crazy?

Either way, I need him to know that while I can't explain it, I know he's not the monster everyone thinks he is. A monster couldn't look at me the way he does. A monster wouldn't keep me warm and safe in his arms. A monster couldn't possibly fill my heart with earnest desire.

Unless, perhaps, I'm a monster too.

"Then tell me, Rae, what do you think you see?" Kharon allows a thin, crescent smile to quirk at the corner of his tightened lips. "Because all I am now is a wretched and cursed old man. You aren't safe here, not with me."

Once more, Kharon turns away, but my fingers quickly catch his jaw, keeping his eyes locked with mine. "You're not going to scare me away, Kharon," I counter, and I watch his eyes soften with relief. "But I need you to be honest with me."

Taking my wrist, he gently pulls his face from my hand, but I quickly twine my fingers with his. Kharon's eyes dart over his shoulder at me, likely surprised by the gesture. Frankly, my newfound boldness shocks me too.

After a tense moment, his posture relaxes, and he blows out a sigh. I don't know if he's relieved or annoyed, but I maintain my grasp on his hand. I came all this way; I must stay my course.

"What do you want to know?"

Okay, here goes nothing. Time to prove I've indeed got a steel pair of lady balls.

"Why did you hold my cousin hostage? Why did you make us think he was dead?"

A small, almost bashful smile lingers at the corner of his mouth, and he laughs, shaking his head. "I see you're not holding in any punches, eh?"

Raising my chin to see newly placed admiration in his eyes, I step forward, squeezing his hand and closing the space between us. "No, Kharon. Tonight, I'm holding nothing back."

Letting out a faint gasp, Kharon's jaw tightens, and his gaze awakens something in me I've never felt before. Unfortunately, I don't have time to revel in the newfound passion budding within me when Kharon grabs his abdomen in pain and tugs himself from my hold.

"Well, that's good a thing. I don't know how much time we have, so I'll make it quick," he states when he recovers from his episode, turning away from me and walking deeper into the cave.

I'm on his heel as he lights more candles and shuffles a few things around on a makeshift stone table next to another pile of silk and satin fabrics. Curiosity flutters within me as I wonder what he's doing with it all, but I temper my interest for now.

"What do you mean we don't have much time, Kharon?"

Huffing, Kharon turns quickly, his eyes clearly surprised to find me standing only an inch away. He breathes hard once more, and I can't help taking a whiff of his intoxicating scent. I wish he would just hold me like he did on the ski lift.

Stepping back to create a little distance between us, Kharon rubs the stubble on his jaw and smiles awkwardly.

"You do see what I've become, right? I mean, ever since your cousin kissed Lux and the Young Lord Elysian was freed, I've turned into an aged old man. Soon, I'll be a walking corpse! You really don't need to hang around for this. Please, just go! I can't bear for you to watch me die—I'm a dead man, Rae!" Kharon spits his words like fire, but the fear I see in his eyes sends tremors through my body.

I never thought I'd see Kharon Nyx afraid.

Does he think the Guard will come back to kill him? Why does he keeping saying he's old? He looks like the same man I've always loved, golden blonde tresses and eyes like a stormy sea. Just looking at Kharon Nyx makes me want to ride the torrent of his waves and drown in the depths of his seas. Sure, he's in his forties and there's an obvious age-gap, but I've never thought of him as old. To me, he's the untold lover of my dreams.

"Don't talk like that, Kharon." I force my abandoned thoughts aside.

Brushing his hands through his hair, he blows out a heap of frustration, his knees buckling. He looks like he's about to faint.

"You don't have to patronize me, Rae. Just go," Kharon sighs, panting hard, as if he's trying to catch his breath. "Let me die in peace."

Kharon has no idea how much his words haunt me. Those

were the last words my mother said when she told my father to take her two wailing children from her deathbed as cancer coursed through her veins. While I'm sure it was harder for her than I could ever imagine, being ripped from her side at ten years old is a pain I never hoped to endure again. Sadly, I didn't even get the chance to bid my father farewell when the drunk driver took him from us only a year after Mother's passing. To make matters worse, arriving here was no better. Melchior's loss came immediately after we arrived.

Maybe it's me. Maybe death follows me wherever I go.

Perhaps. I don't know. What I do know is I will not leave Kharon to uncertain fate. Whether it be the hand of Lord Marchand's guards or any other, I refuse to stand idly by, allowing death to have its way.

"No, Kharon, I'm not leaving you," I start as I wrap my arms around his waist. He winces in pain.

"Please, Rae, you shouldn't see whatever comes next. I'd rather just die. Please!" Kharon pleads once more, grief-stricken, his eyes a river of tears. "After the pain I've caused you, it's what I deserve."

My eyes well with tears, but I can't break down now. *He needs me.* Watching him writhe in agony both confounds me and raises a protectiveness I don't understand. Keeping my grip firm, I rub his back, hopeful I'm providing an ounce of comfort.

Laughing as though it hurts, Kharon looks up at me and cracks a dim smile. "I guess you won't let me die in peace, huh?"

"No, Kharon, I won't, but if you let me, I'd rather be your peace."

Four

KHARON

Little does Rae know, just her presence is all the peace I could ever ask for. Why she remains insistent to be at my side after my trespasses, I can't understand, but I'm done asking her to leave.

I want her by my side. I need her here.

Even if the next breath I take is to be my last, at least the care in her eyes will be the closest I get to paradise. For as much as I wanted a life with her, a dying man can't be picky. I'll take whatever she's willing to give.

"You give me more peace than you could ever know, Rae," I mumble, almost incoherently, and I doubt she understands my garble as I grit my teeth through the aching pain.

Dropping to her knees, Rae helps me sit against the wall. "Kharon, please -- tell me what's happening to you! Did the Guard do something? Why are you in so much pain?"

Grunting, I force out a small laugh. "Please," I seethe, pushing myself upright. Looking up at Rae, my heart nearly melts as a sliver of moonlight pierces through the darkness of the cave, illuminating her in its pale glow. It suits her well. She certainly is a bright light in my darkness. "Those wretched wolves and vampires of the Guard can't hurt what they can't see." I laugh once more.

Rae's mouth twists in the cutest way, and I know I've confused her. "Kharon, you aren't making sense."

"Well, if your uncle or the Guard knew anything of worth about the Netherworld, they'd understand the power of onyx." Picking up a small velvet box, I offer it to Rae.

Hesitant, her hands shake as she takes the box from me. Casting a wary glance at me, she extends the box back to me without looking inside. "Isn't that the same ring box I saw you offer as a proposal to my cousin?"

I want to laugh, but I don't think it wise as I register the darting glare she's giving me. "Ah, so I take it Win never told you there was no proposal."

She frowns. "No proposal, huh? So, you just carry this thing around on the off chance you're getting hitched?" Rae counters, shaking the box between her fingers.

"Open it, Rae!" I demand. I won't die having her believe for another minute I ever loved her cousin. I may have pursued her, believing doing so would save my sister, but I *never* loved Winter Elysian.

I can tell she wants to protest, but I'm sure Rae sees she's not the only one with a sharp glance.

She does as I instruct, and she looks up at me confused when she sees the onyx sand inside. "What's this?"

"Well, where I come from, the Fates use it for protection and safety. My sister, Moirai, is a Fate, and she ensured I had plenty when I came here. I used it in the ballroom to, um, make myself invisible."

"So that's why they couldn't find you earlier?" Rae quietly says, putting the pieces together. I only nod in agreement as a shooting pain bolts through me again. "I don't understand. Why were you going to share this with Winter? Were you going to tell her everything?"

I sigh. Everything in me hates where this conversation is going, but it's best we get all the cards on the table.

"Well, yes and no." My tone is flat as I watch Rae trail her fingers along the trim of the small box. "No, I didn't think it was time to tell her everything, but I wanted to show her the box to say that if we took our relationship to the next level, I could tell her about it, about me. To free Melchior, Winter would have to love the holder of the obol while knowing the truth. There was never a ring, Rae."

My heart nearly plummets to the floor as I watch Rae's eyes pool with tears.

"So, you did want to be with Win. You wanted to tell *her* everything about you," Rae tearfully mutters. Sighing hard, she brushes a stray tear from her cheek. Taking a deep breath, she looks up at me and shoves the box into my chest. I'm almost surprised by the sheer force she uses to plunge it forward, but I know I deserve every bit of the pain she inflicts. "I guess it's a good thing I know how you really feel!"

Her words hit hard, but as she makes to leave my side, I use whatever strength remains in me to yank her back. "No, Rae, you can't even imagine how I feel. I only told you my plan. I never said I loved Win."

"There's nothing wrong with my hearing, Kharon! I clearly heard you say you wanted to take your relationship with her to the next level—what kind of fool do you take me for?"

Ripping herself away from my grasp, she jumps up, and I wish I had the strength to stop her. "You're not a fool, Rae!" I shout to her back as she snatches one of my satin fabrics from the ground and wraps it around herself. Working myself up from the floor, I know this is my only chance to make her understand. "What would you do if Ross' life was in danger? To what end would you go to ensure his life?"

Stopping mid-motion, Rae spins on her heel, her eyes tinged with anger. "So, it's not enough that you make me look like a drooling idiot, fawning after you while you declare your love to my cousin, or even what you did to Melchior—now you're threatening *my twin*? Really? If you try to lay a hand on him, I promise you, your onyx sand won't protect you from me. If you even—"

"It's my sister, Rae," I belt out with my remaining strength. Curiosity fills her face, but I don't give her the opportunity to ask more. "My sister, Moirai, is being held hostage by the Changelings. We both are—but Moirai even more so. The Changelings sent me here as one of many to breach the borders beyond the Netherworld. When Melchior found my obol, the Changelings decided to use him as a pawn. I was told the only way for my sister and me to free ourselves of their curse was to do two things: earn the wealth of the land—hence the grain of truth of the cursed ferrymen being bound by a coin. In the Netherworld, it's impossible to earn enough to secure our own passage, but here, it's possible."

Dropping the satin covering on the ground, Rae takes a few steps toward me. Her darkened glare tells me I haven't regained her trust, but I'm thankful to merely have her attention. "And the second?" she asks with her arms folded, a fatigued lilt in her voice, nearly mirroring my own.

"Find true love," I reveal, pausing enough to watch her face softly settle away her scowl. Her brows lift, and her mouth parts so slowly, everything in me wishes I were the wind between her lips. I've never been more jealous of air than I am at this moment. As much as I loathe bringing Rae into the chaos of my world, it's time she learned the truth. I steady myself against the wall to continue. "As the holder of the obol, I was tasked with gaining the affection of one who cared for Melchior. Only their kiss would set him free from his prison and end both mine and my sister's servitude to the Changelings."

Rae's lips twist slightly as she takes a few steps closer to me. "But Melchior is my cousin and I love—"

Leaning forward, my thoughts hurl like thunder from my mouth. "But he is not your blood, Rae!" I rush my words out. "Believe me, I tried, Rae, I tried." I sigh, pushing myself back against the wall, slowly slumping back to the ground. I hate being curt with her, but the pain is white-hot inside me, and I don't know how much time I have left.

"What do you mean you tried, Kharon?"

A small smile creeps up my face as I point to my stone table. "Look on the mirror tray with the blue satin ribbon." Keeping her sights on me, Rae takes small steps toward the table. Untying the blue ribbon, her eyes grow wide as she stares back at me.

Surprise fills her face as she holds her hair in her palm. "Is this —is this my hair?"

"Yes, Rae, it's yours. I brought it here on the day we were trapped on the lift. I needed to test it, to see if you were the one. Everything in me hoped you were—but it was revealed you were not of Elysian blood."

Rae's eyes grow wide but quickly narrow as she drops her hair to the ground. "Oh, so when you found out I wasn't an Elysian, you just moved on to my cousin. Really?"

"Look, Rae, I know it was deceitful. I understand if you can never forgive me. If it were only my life, if it were just about me, I'd endure whatever hell necessary, as long as I could spend a day in heaven with you at my side!" Once more, Rae's face softens, and tears pool in her eyes again.

She's speechless. Good. Perhaps I can finally make her understand.

"It's like I asked you before. What would you endure to save your brother? For me, it's all for Moirai—for my sister. We are all that remain of the House of Erebus. We lost the others long ago to the savage lands of the Netherworld and the dark witchery of the Changelings. I couldn't bear to lose her as I'd lost the others. I know I may appear a smug, selfish fool—and I may indeed be all those things -- but my sister is all I have in both this world and the next. I couldn't lose the only person who ever loved me."

Kneeling beside me again, Rae takes my face in her hand and smiles. Thick teardrops petal down to her chin, and my heart aches at the thought of not only failing my sister but missing an opportunity to wipe away the tears flooding the face of the most beautiful creature I've ever seen.

"I'd do anything for Ross," she answers in a tone so sure and sweet, my heart melts. "In case you haven't figured it out by now, why I'm risking it all—it's because Moirai isn't the only one to ever love you, you fool!" Shaking her head, Rae laughs, and I feel something perk inside me. "I love you, Kharon. I've always loved you."

Warmth fills the entirety of me, and a twinge of vigor reignites parts of me I've only wanted to share with Rae. Before I can reply, Rae pulls me close and crushes her mouth to mine.

A kiss before dying, how sweet.

Five

RAE

THIS IS NOT how I expected our first kiss to go, but for the life of me, I refuse to stop now.

I never expected to be the one initiating my first kiss with Kharon Nyx, but here I am, owning my heart, as my brother Ross would say.

My heart. What a muddled mess it is!

A mess because, despite everything Kharon has done, nothing changes how I feel about him. The way his lips lock with my own, I know something has changed. *Me.* A better woman wouldn't give a thought to a man who expressed even faux interest for a cousin she considers a sister.

I am not a better woman.

I am a woman who has stayed too long in the shadows.

I am a woman who, for too long, hid her heart in a vault, waiting for someone else to unlock it.

Now, in this moment, I know I alone hold the key to my heart. I will no longer sit idly by, waiting to be swept away by some romanticized knight in shining armor. No, give me the monster. Give me the one who haunts my dreams and torments the deepest parts of my soul. I want the one who walks in the company of darkness, with me as his guiding light.

As Kharon's delicious tongue swirls in my mouth, I finally realize why I held myself back from pursuing what I want—who I want. I was afraid those I love would see me differently. Who would think the petite, bashful, freckled girl would willingly give her heart to the villain of the story?

What will they say when they learn there may be a monster within me as well?

It doesn't matter. I suppose it never did.

Slowly, Kharon pulls away from our kiss as he holds my face in his palm. "Well, that was unexpected," he laughs and my eyes land on the perfection of his smile. His stormy eyes dig into my own, and I feel a gathering of wetness at my thighs that I've only ever felt when Kharon was near—but so much more now.

I don't know what brazen force has overtaken me, but I've got one foot in the boat now, so I might as well go with it. "Maybe for you," I whisper into his warm palm. Kharon's eyes darken with a glint of surprise. "The moment I saw you tonight, I had every intention of doing just that."

And perhaps more...but I'll keep that to myself.

For now.

Six

KHARON

Everything about Rae Vereen in this moment is unexpected. Though I've spent long nights fantasizing about what it would be like to hold her in my arms, what it would feel like to have her soft lips upon my own, the fantasy hardly compares to the reality.

Despite everything I've done, Rae looks at me as if she would surrender everything to me in this very moment, and it speeds the beating of my heart to a pace rivaled by Mercury himself. Even more, I feel parts of me I thought were dying only moments ago reviving with a vigor that can only be placed at her feet.

What is she doing to me?

Gazing into her piercing hazel eyes as her luscious mouth lingers open in desire, I wish with all my being that I was the man she deserved. She deserves better than the wretchedness I have to offer.

Pushing myself up, I try to muster the strength to stand and get her perfect face away from me before I do something we'll both regret. "You deserve better," I mumble, the thoughts in my mind flying right out of my mouth before I can rein them in.

"I deserve you." Rae's reply is quick as her hands rest firm on my shoulders, preventing me from moving.

Looking at her, the glint of defiance in her eyes kindles a flame in me I thought was extinguished long ago. How she can stomach the sight of me right now perplexes me, but I feel my own defenses waning.

Still, I refuse to give in. Where I come from, no one just surrenders. What if this a counterattack of sorts? Maybe the Guard or Elysian sent her to subdue me. "How can you say that? After everything I did to you, to your family. There's no way you can forgive me so easily." My words come out harsher than I intend, but when the softened curves of her mouth straighten into a thin line, I know I'm testing her patience.

"Wow, Kharon," she says, leaning away from me as her eyes search my face. She's wary of me. Good. She should be. "Are you really not accustomed to someone loving you in spite of you? Have you never experienced forgiveness?" Rae's gentle tone stirs something strange in me again.

"But how can you forgive me?" I don't deserve her forgiveness. *I don't deserve her.*

"Because despite everything—your half-hearted pursuit of my cousin, the years you've spent watching me when you thought I didn't notice, the stolen moments when you'd look at me like I was the only woman in the world—I always knew there was something between us. After what you shared about Moirai, I understand the position you were in, but even more, I'm not just forgiving you—I'm forgiving myself."

Watching Rae's tearful gaze as she confesses her affection for me, my hands quickly find her face, catching the tiny droplets as they fall to her chin. "I don't understand. What do you need forgiveness for?"

Once more, Rae leans into my palm, closing her eyes, savoring my touch. "For waiting this long to finally show you how I feel."

Seven

RAE

Kharon's eyes flash with a flame-like glow, and before I can finish my thought, his mouth is on mine.

This time, it's Kharon, not me, leading the way. His hands palm my face, desperation seeping through his kiss, lulling my body to the brink of surrender. As our tongues twine together, I'm almost overtaken with the expert way Kharon gently nips my bottom lip, as if he wants to consume me whole.

Oh, how I wish he would!

Raking his hands through my hair, Kharon fists a handful of my curls, holding me steady as he pulls away just enough to gaze deeply into my eyes. My body tells me he's looking for a hint of indecision. He needs to know if I want to go the distance, but I'm letting my body lead the way. It's about time my body finally got the attention it's long deserved. Kharon will find no objection from me.

Logic be damned.

"Please, Kharon," I moan, tilting my head back, giving him more than an eyeful of my cleavage. Grunting, Kharon pulls me back to him, gluing his mouth to mine as his hands explore my curves.

Running his hands along my breasts and my waist as our kiss deepens, the wetness between my thighs gushes, as if his touch alone ignited my climax. I quake in his grip, and Kharon smirks a wickedly sexy grin as he looks at me briefly before plunging his face between my breasts.

"You don't know how long I've wanted to do this," he growls into my bustline. Whimpering moans are all I have in reply as I wish there were a better, more alluring way to rip this gown from my body. "Rae," Kharon breathes my name, looking up at me through darkened eyes. "Are you sure this is what you want? If we do this, there's no going back."

He looks at me as if my next words could be the death of him, and I allow a small smile as I roll into the thick pile of silk fabrics at my side.

"Kharon, this is all I ever wanted. *You* are all I ever wanted—all I want," I say, desperate for his touch.

Kharon's hooded glare darkens even more, the flame resting behind his irises flickering again as he leans toward me. This time, I notice he doesn't look as pained as before.

As he slowly unbuttons his shirt, my eyes land square on his sculpted chest and perfect abs. If I didn't know better, I'd think he was either born perfect or was a Greek sculpture come to life. Making his way to me, a bright glow hovers around him as the shimmering sheen radiating from his body illuminates the dark cave. Darting his eyes quickly to me, he looks genuinely surprised. Rubbing his hands along his biceps and chest, it's as if this were the first time he saw himself.

The wonder in his eyes puzzles me, and I feel like I'm missing something. "Kharon, what's wrong?"

Smiling as the brightness around him slowly fades, he looks down at me as if he just won a prize. "That's just it, Rae. Nothing. Nothing is wrong—at least, not anymore, and it's all because of you!"

Eight

KHARON

I ALMOST FEEL like myself again. How, I'm not quite sure, but I know Rae Vereen is responsible for it all.

As the luminous glow dissipates, I am full of awe. Gone is the wrinkled, mole and boil-ridden skin that made me grotesque monster in front of everyone at the cotillion. It's as if the veil of the beast I'd become has been lifted, my true self revealed.

Puzzled, Rae looks up at me with her big bright eyes, and it takes every ounce of my restraint not to take her in my arms. I need to know for sure.

"Kharon?" Rae says, rising to her knees as I make my way to Moirai's onyx stone. I need answers.

"Rae, I promise, I'll explain everything to you, but I need you to be honest with me."

"Of course," she answers, searching my face.

Patting my face, I'm surprised to no longer find sagging skin or sunken eyes, but Rae stares at me as though nothing has changed. "How do I look to you? I mean, do I look like some old, decrepit man? Like I did at the cotillion?"

"The cotillion? Are you really stopping to ask me how you look? I mean—"

"Please, Rae, I promise this isn't about vanity. Seriously, what do you see?" I need to know I'm not losing my mind.

Standing up, Rae closes the distance between us. Tracing her petite fingers along my chest and abs, she hums, fluttering her eyes up at me through her perfect lashes. "I see you, Kharon. I've always seen you." Slowly, Rae's hands reach my face, cupping my chin.

Just her touch calms my angst, soothing the trepidation brewing within me.

Her words shoot straight to my manhood, and it's taking everything in me not to throw her back on the pile of silks and satins behind her. Just her touch invigorates me in ways that only hours ago, I thought myself incapable.

Before I have a chance to reply, Moirai's bright light shines through the stone and her veiled form appears. "Greetings, brother!" Moirai calls to me, startling Rae as she jumps back into my arms. As I pull her into my hold, Rae grunts and looks up at me in shock when she senses my hardness now pressed at her backside. "I hope I'm not interrupting you," Moirai continues, slightly distracting me.

"Greetings, sister," I start, rubbing Rae's shoulders, hopeful to ease the concern I sense building within her. "I'd like you to meet someone," I announce with a puffed chest as I finally introduce my sister to the most beautiful woman I've ever known.

"No introductions are necessary." Moirai's bright tone shines through the onyx stone, and I can only imagine my lovely sister's smile stretching ear to ear. "With the way your eyes are dancing, I know this must be the Rae Vereen you've spoken so fondly of."

Rae looks over her shoulder at me as a bashful smile crosses her face. Kissing the top of Rae's head, I wrap my arms around her as she nuzzles herself deeper into my embrace. It feels so good to hold her.

A small chuckle escapes me, and I'm surprised at the lighter turn the night has taken. "You are quite right, Moirai—as always."

"Yes, but that is not what you want to know, is it, brother? You want to know why the cursed stench of death brought on by the Changelings is leaving your body?"

Rae steps aside, looking back and forth between me and Moirai, concern filling her face. "Kharon, what is your sister talking about? What does she mean by death?"

The worry in Rae's eyes pierces my heart. I want nothing but to bring her back to the impassioned precipice she clung to only moments ago, but I can't go further without understanding what's happening to me.

"Moirai, please, no riddles," I begin, all too familiar with the furtive speech of the Fates and Changelings alike. I know my sister can't help it. Fates like her don't typically give straightforward answers, and Changelings, confounded by this earthbound plane, use language more in line with a parable or limerick than the fluid sentence structure of men.

"Well, Rae Vereen," Moirai answers, keeping her attention on Rae, ignoring me. "Once the obol was stolen from Kharon and your cousin Melchior set free, the curse the Changelings put on my brother was unleashed—quickening his age, inevitably speeding him to death's door."

Horrorstruck, Rae turns back to me, clutching my arm. "No!"

she cries. "Please don't let them do anything to him. I know he was only trying to save you, not hurt Melchior! I can explain it. I'll make them understand. Please!"

"Ah, what a pure heart she has, dear brother," Moirai sighs. "It is the love and purity of her heart that is freeing you from their wretched curse."

Squeezing my arm, Rae's tearful eyes stare up at me. My heart leaps at the care I see laced in the small smile curved at the corner of her perfect, apricot-hued lips.

"That is why she alone can see you for who you are—not for who they made you to be," Moirai adds, and all the puzzle pieces slowly snap into place in my mind.

Once Melchior was free, my body shriveled into an unsightly, decaying old man. The curse of the Changelings upon the Sons of Erebus was clear: without true love, we would fade from existence. If I were still in the Netherworld, such a fate would place me in servitude as a ferryman of the Underworld—a collector of souls. Here on an earthbound plane, I would simply fade away and die.

"Rae, when I asked earlier how I looked to you—you said you saw me. Earlier at the cotillion the lot of them were horrorstruck by the mere sight of me, but not you. You saw me—the real me. If what my sister says is true, that can only mean one thing."

Wiping the trail of tears flowing to her chin, Rae looks up at me with hopeful eyes. "What, Kharon? What does it mean?"

Taking her face in my hand, I smile. I can't believe I didn't understand it before, but looking at her, the truth is plain to see. "It means you are, in fact, my true love. Only a love as true as yours can see me not for what some curse would make me out to be, but for who I am—for who you deserve."

"Who is that, Kharon? Who do I deserve?" Rae asks, leaning into my palm.

"I am yours, Rae Vereen, all yours. That is, if you'll have me," I reply, pressing my forehead to hers.

"Why do you think I'm here, Kharon? I've been waiting for what feels like my whole life to have you—I'll never let you go."

Nine

RAE

GENTLY PRESSING his mouth to mine, Kharon lifts my chin as he softly covers my lips with his. There is a sweetness in his kiss, different than before, not lapping me like a starved man as he did earlier. His pace is soothing, lulling my body back to a place of surrender I've only ever felt in his embrace.

I love it.

"You don't have to worry, Rae. I'm not going anywhere," Kharon whispers against my mouth.

"But what about my family?" I ask, looking up at his tender and doting gaze. "How will we make them understand you were never trying to hurt Melchior?" As much as I want what Kharon and I have to be accepted, I know my family will disapprove.

Just as Kharon parts his lips to reply, a light from the onyx stone shines brightly, turning our attention back to Moirai. "Well, I don't think you'll have as much trouble as you think. Melchior knows firsthand Kharon never meant to deceive you."

"What? How is that possible? I thought Melchior was a prisoner."

"Yes, Rae, but Melchior was never *my* prisoner," Kharon begins, brushing his hands through my hair.

"Is that what you were trying to say before? At the cotillion?"

Nodding, Kharon smiles and kisses my forehead before pulling me to his side and turning back toward Moirai's stone. "That is exactly what I was trying to say at the cotillion, but after everyone believed I imprisoned Melchior, no one heard anything I had to say."

"Except for me," I breathe back, looking up at Kharon and noticing the more youthful features framing his face. Gone are the hardened lines around his eyes and mouth. Even the gray etching of his hairline has faded into fuller, wavy, golden blonde tresses.

Smiling back at me, he tugs me tighter at the waist. "More than anyone, Rae, you've always seen me. I know that now. You didn't see the decrepit being I'd become; you've only seen the better part of me."

"Yes, brother," Moirai begins. "Between Melchior and Rae, the Elysians will yet understand that your actions were engineered by the Changelings alone. Melchior will speak up for you; just give him time. If need be, remind him of me. While he was in the dark prism, I did what I could to make his stay more—um, palatable."

Raising his brow and slightly stiffening his posture, Kharon steps forward. "What do you mean?"

As she laughs, the light in Moirai's stone brightens once more. "Melchior will understand," she cuts him off. "Just as I understand

I must now leave you two to rekindle the flame I saw lit only moments ago."

Both Kharon and I share shy smiles and I quickly dart my eyes to my feet, slightly embarrassed.

"But sister?" Kharon counters once more.

"No, brother. I have spent too much time here. Since they no longer have power over you, they will come for me. I must go!"

"Moirai, wait!" Kharon pleads, breaking from my side and moving closer to the stone. "This isn't over! You promised me if I followed the Changelings' order to come to this world, I'd also set you free. I will not rest until you are!"

"Yes, brother, and as a Fate, I hold my word as true. I indeed told you to follow their lead. In doing so, you finally have your true love—the one to set you free. Now so is Melchior free."

Kharon's posture shifts and a grim gaze lingers at his brow. "But you told me to pursue Winter, not Rae," he grits in a whisper through his teeth, like he hates himself for uttering the words.

Although hearing this should make me uncomfortable, I'm not. Deep down, I've always known Kharon never wanted Win, despite Uncle El's persistence. I suppose that's why he never formally proposed.

Sighing, Moirai's shadow shifts a bit as her light flickers dimly. "Had it not been for your pursuit of Winter, her true love, the hybrid, Luxor Decanter, would not have been driven to free Melchior. By stealing your obol, he effectively broke the Changelings' hold over you. From there, Rae had all the provocation necessary to pursue her heart, for only Rae's love could free you from death."

Kharon glances at me for a moment before continuing. "What about you?"

"Dear brother, put your mind at ease and stay the course. You know as well as I that, as a Fate, I can only point you in the right direction. My freedom still rests in your hands. As you and Rae conquer all that comes next, my freedom shall indeed be won. For now, Kharon, take pleasure in the one thing of which your heart has too long been deprived: love. Don't do so for yourself alone, but for me, as nothing brings me more joy than seeing your happiness fulfilled. You, Kharon, of all the Sons of Erebus, deserve it most. So, with this, I bid you farewell for now. Know this: I too, love you, my brother, and while it will only be but a breath for me, not long from now, I shall once more behold your face."

With her parting words, the light of the onyx stone fades to black. Pounding his hand against the wall, Kharon growls. Seeing him like this, I know his heart breaks for his sister. Even more, I now understand just how much she means to him. Everything he did, he did for her. Being a twin, I understand the depth of a sibling's love more than most.

Slowly trailing my hands up Kharon's arm and running my fingers along the brawn muscles of his back, I hope my touch soothes the ache I see brewing in his eyes. It's the same ache I saw at the cotillion. It wasn't seeing Win with Lux that was vexing him as much as everyone believed. The source of his pain was thinking that without Win, he and his sister would remain both cursed and hostage.

I don't know how I'll do it, but in my heart, I know my sole purpose in this moment is to relieve the vexing in his heart. Although the flame I see in his eyes should scare me, for him, I am willing to burn.

Ten

KHARON

Rae's touch is the only thing holding me together. I want nothing more than to see my sister freed from the Changelings' hold, but one thing is true: I'll never stop searching for a way to free Moirai. Even if it means I have to return to the Netherworld through hell's door—I will free her from the wretched Changelings.

"Kharon." The sweetness of Rae's voice as she says my name sends a signal straight to my manhood. When I turn to see her desirous gaze, I feel steel strength rise at my crotch. "It's okay. We'll find a way to save Moirai—together. You don't have to do this alone. You have me now."

The wonderfulness of this woman knows no end. She is everything I ever needed. She is perfect.

"And you have me," I say, watchful of the rise and fall of her cleavage. Memories of the taste of her on my tongue has my mind racing. "Whatever comes next, we do it together. That includes getting your family to accept us, and whatever I have to do to prove to you that there has not nor shall there ever be another woman for me. There is only you. Do you understand? We do this—"

"Together," Rae finishes my sentiment as I take her hand in mine.

Staring into her hazel eyes, I can't help admiring the perfect placement of the freckles along her cheeks and the lovely way her sandy brown, wavy hair frames her face. Right now, though, it's the alluring call of her petite and curvaceous figure sending me into overdrive.

Instinct guides my arm around her waist, pulling her tight against me. Her eyes grow wide as she feels me jutting against her abdomen, but I don't give her time to respond as I fist her hair, craning her neck up for a quick kiss.

This time, I need her to know to whom she now belongs. I need her to know that all of what I am is hers.

Rae makes no move to push me from her side as she saddles her leg to my hip, lifting her gown from the floor, allowing me to hold her thigh at my waist.

I need more.

Pulling her other leg up, I straddle her at my waist, just above my cock as I carry her to the fabrics laying at the center floor. Easing Rae to the ground, I marvel at how her caramel complexion glistens in the moonlight.

Keeping her legs wide, I trail my hand up her dress, enjoying the soft, delicate touch of her skin. She feels like silk.

It doesn't take me long to get to the place I've only imagined in my dreams. "May I touch you here?" I ask, gently tapping the small piece of lace fabric shielding me from what I truly desire.

Pushing her hips up, Rae bites her lip before grabbing my head and pulling me into another kiss. "Please, Kharon, it's yours," she whines beneath me, breathless.

"Has anyone ever touched you here?" I tap once more, and the mewling noises she's making under my grip almost have me exploding in my trousers.

"No one," she groans, running her hands through her hair in the sexiest way possible. "I was waiting for you."

At her confession, I slowly slip my finger beneath the lace fabric, and I nearly get goosebumps when I feel the soft perfection of her. The wetness I feel at her entrance sends me into a frenzy, and my member almost bucks out of my pants as her sweet nectar coats my finger.

"I can't wait anymore, Rae. Your honey is calling me. I need to see you."

Lifting two of the silks at my sides, I hold them over Rae's gown, motioning my hands up and down her body as she writhes beneath me, enjoying each stroke of my touch. Pulling the fabrics from her body, she gasps when she sees she's now totally naked before me.

"How did you do that?" she asks, her face blushing red.

"It's just a little trick of mine, one I'll share with you later. Right now, I need to look at you." Batting her eyes up at me, there's an innocence in her gaze that makes me want to repent every sin I've ever committed and vow to be a better man. There's also a glint of confident seduction there, and I now see Rae Vereen is quite comfortable baring herself to me.

"Like what you see?" she adds, parting her legs just enough for me to glimpse her opening.

She is a goddess!

"Not like. *Love*," I grunt, palming the hard bulging in my

pants. "Need to taste." I sound like a caveman, but I don't care. Neither does she, apparently, as she places her hands on my shoulders, pushing me down.

Once I'm face to face with her depths, I inhale her scent before plunging my tongue inside her. Swirling, twisting, and nipping at her sensitive skin, I'm intent on having her nectar flood my face. Rae's honey is heaven, and so is she as she clamps down on the sides of my head with her knees. I fear my last moment on earth may be partaking of the most delicious treasure I have ever known.

"Kharon!" Rae screams as I feel her pulsating on my tongue.

As much as I have every intent on her releasing on my length, I'll let her have this one. With the way she's screaming incoherently and holding me hostage against her sweetness, I know she needed this more than she'll ever say. She can have as many as she wants, as long as she has them with me.

Eleven

RAE

I DON'T KNOW if I just spoke in an unknown language or not, but Kharon's tongue is masterful.

Truly, I had no idea a tongue could do to me what Kharon's just did. I can only hope he does it again.

Slowly moving from between my legs, I see the smoldering haze Kharon had from before still lingers. With a wicked smirk, he licks his lips as he wipes my arousal from his chin. "Sweet. I knew you'd taste sweet. Thank you for sharing yourself with me."

"And what about you?" I ask, daring myself to be brave as I sit up on my elbows.

Tilting his head, his wavy hair falls to his cheekbones, and he smirks once more. "What about me?"

I inwardly groan. "Will you share yourself with me?"

Kharon's eyes grow wide, mixed with lust and shock. "Do you think you're ready, my little honeycomb?"

"There's only one way to find out," I say, lingering my gaze on his waistline. Thankfully, Kharon wastes no time dropping his trousers to the floor, but I'm almost unprepared to see the glistening monster aimed at me.

Slowly making my way to him, my instincts drive me forward, once more leaving logic behind. Logic says I'm too inexperienced to know how to please a mammoth of a man like Kharon, but in this moment, I'll choose to follow my body's lead.

"You don't have to do this, Rae. I don't want you doing anything you don't want to do."

"I've never wanted anything more," I answer, taking the width of him in my hands as I bring him to my mouth.

As I use my tongue to taste the sheen already awaiting me along his tip, Kharon sucks in a breath, once more taking my hair in his hands. "Damn, Rae, how did you know what I needed?"

"Because you're mine," I speak directly to the hardness of him hovering at my bottom lip.

Taking him in my mouth, I loosen my jaw, hopeful to capture the fullness of him as his sweet, salty flavor explodes across my tongue. Allowing Kharon to thrust himself back and forth, his grunts grow more desperate as curses roar out of him with each stroke.

I'm not sure if he's going to explode, but I prepare my mouth for him just in case. He tastes so good.

"No, baby, I'm not going to come in your mouth. Not for our first time." Releasing my hair, Kharon pulls out and pushes me back down onto the pillowy, satin mound behind me. "All of me. In you. Now!"

At his words, I pull my knees to my chest, opening myself for him. I've never gone the distance before, but this is all I ever wanted. I have no idea how he plans to fit that monster inside of me, but I'm more than willing to allow him safe passage.

"I'm not using protection," Kharon says, gripping his rock-hard shaft. "I need to feel every bit of you."

If he were any other man, the notion would sound arrogant, but he has no idea how badly I want him.

"You are my protection," I answer, widening my legs. "I need to feel everything."

Kharon's eyes flash bright as he smiles. "Rae, you are perfect," he groans with another quick kiss. "It may hurt and I'm sorry," Kharon adds, keeping himself aligned with my entrance.

"I'm not," I reply, reaching down and placing my hand over his. "We do this together."

"Mmm...together," he breathes, slipping slowly inside me. "Fu—Rae, you're so tight! Baby, you gotta let me in!" he roars. "I don't want to hurt you, beautiful."

The mewling sounds coming from me as he inches deeper and deeper become more desperate with each thrust. "Just do it, Kharon!" I moan back. "I don't care if it hurts. I want to feel all of you, baby! Make it hurt! Please!" I beg.

"Damn, Rae!" Kharon grunts, thrashing his length inside me. "Can you feel it now? Do you know how much I craved this sweetness? Now that I've tasted you—now that I'm in you—I am all you'll ever have. No one will take you from me."

"I'm yours!" I whine as Kharon plows into me, driving deeper and deeper, as if he means to reach my heart. I hope he knows he already has.

"And I am yours, Rae."

As he thrusts himself deeper, I become completely undone. Kharon clamps his hands at my throat, squeezing slightly as he utters enchanting words too beautiful for me to comprehend. His eyes flash with flame-like fire, and it's as though I can see into his soul. All darkness. All pain. All fire.

There's something else, peering from behind the blazing inferno locking my gaze. If I didn't know better, I'd swear I saw waterfalls and the calming view of a river flowing over rocks. All I know is the most alluring man straddled between heaven and hell is hitting my peaks, ripping my virginity to shreds.

And I love it.

Who knew getting fucked by the Ferryman could feel like paradise?

Pulling out of me, Kharon holds himself firm, admiring the glistening wetness and tinge of pink covering him. My heart melts knowing it was to Kharon I gave my most precious gift. I've waited forever to give it to him.

"On your knees!" Kharon orders me, flipping me over with one hand. "You told me to make it hurt. I hope you're ready for what you asked for.

Twelve

KHARON

Rae wastes no time hiking her ass in the air, revealing the sweet pearl that has my mind on edge. All I can think about is getting back inside her. Nothing else matters.

Looking at her perfectly round bottom, I smack it, watching it jiggle for me. Peering over her shoulder at me, the desire seeping from her pores is not lost on me as she bites her lip, enjoying the effect she has on me as her eyes glance down at the stiffness I now hold in my hands.

"What a pretty sight," I say with another smack on her other cheek. Staring at her glistening entrance makes me ravenous. "I plan to see you like this at least once a day for the rest of our lives, Rae."

Raising her brow, she bites her lip, toying with me. "The rest of our lives?" Smiling at me over her shoulder again, Rae coos the sexiest chuckle I've ever heard, and it only makes me harder.

Taking her hair in my hand, I gently yank her back a little and she smirks. I know she delights in a little tussle and play, but I need to remind her how serious I am. "The rest of our lives," I groan.

I slap the hardness of me against her entrance, and she whimpers but arches her back, allowing me to see more of her opening. A man can only take so much teasing. As I drive into her once more, she cries out, as I don't go slow as I did initially. Gasping, she moans as her hands clench the fabric at her sides.

"You told me to make it hurt! So this is what you get!" I roar, feeling like a king as I grip her hips, plowing my way deeper and deeper into her.

"K--Kharon!" she stammers, breathless as her ass bounces against me with each stroke. I could stay back here forever.

"If you keep showing me what's mine, I'll take it!"

"Take it, Kharon! Please, take it!"

Another growl escapes me as my need for her grows unquenchable. I haven't had sex in over a decade. With the exception of the few times I've relieved myself to the thought of Rae, like after our time together on the ski lift, I'm full and desperate for release, but my iron clad member has no thoughts of surrender. In fact, it feels like I'm growing with each stroke.

If this pace continues, we'll never stop, and that's fine with me.

"I need you so much Rae! I need this sweet, sweet, little pearl."

"It's yours, Kharon." Rae wiggles a bit and I feel her pulsing around me.

"Oh, what a greedy little thing you are. Look at you coming again all over me! I need you to come again, sweet girl."

I slowly pull out of her as she shouts, convulsing beneath me as her nectar runs down her thighs.

"Ahh... Kharon," she moans, her eyes clouded with passion.

"I've got you open baby, so there's no need to stop. I need more of you!" I am delirious for everything she is. Part of me wants to take it easy on her, but when she rolls over and opens her arms to me, I know she's just as insatiable as me.

"My turn on top," she smiles with hooded eyes. Taking me in her arms, Rae kisses my forehead and rolls me on my back. Tossing her petite legs over my waist, she hovers over me, teasing my tip with her already slick entrance. Casting me an enchanting smile, her gaze pulls me in, and I'm lost in the wonderfulness of Rae Vereen. Rae wiggles back and forth, as I hold myself against her opening, awaiting permission to enter.

"So, you said you need more?" she teases me, gyrating, careful not to allow more than she can handle.

Her words send more vigor to my core, and I grow harder than I thought possible. "Take your time baby. You don't want to—fu--!"

My words become unintelligible as Rae slides masterfully down on me, whimpering as she does, her body continuing to pulsate around me. I glide my hands from her hips to her slender waist, landing on her breasts as Rae bucks and grinds, as if I were her personal mechanical bull.

She's riding me as if she's done so before.

Perhaps in her dreams.

I know she has in mine.

It's the hypnotic way her perfect, perky breasts bounce in my face that make me want to surrender my full will to her and her alone.

"Is this what you wanted, Kharon?" she asks, trailing her hands along my chest. "You wanted to see what I looked like bouncing on your lap?" Rae moans into my mouth and nips my lip before tossing her head back, allowing her wavy tresses to flow wild down her shoulders.

"Yes, Rae, yes!" I growl as she grinds deep, her juices running between my thighs. I am thankful for her rhythmic motion, and I don't want her to stop.

"I—I—I love you, Kharon! I love you!" she yells as my hands remain steady at her hips and I thrust upward, sending the fullness of me into her depths.

Like a volcano, I erupt inside Rae, filling her with more than I thought possible. Holding her hips, I control our motion, as she, too, meets her climax once more. With harmonious melody, we call out the other's name in a love song so sweet, so perfect, I know it's meant just for us.

While this isn't the first orgasm for either one of us, this time feels different than before.

Then it hits me: we're finally doing it together.

Thirteen

RAE

With my face planted on his chest and his arms wrapped around me, I have no doubt all the comforts of home can be found in Kharon's embrace.

There is no place I'd rather be than right here, in his arms.

During long days and nights, I dreamed what it would be like to be completely surrendered to him. Yet, no matter how hot and steamy my dreams became, the fantasy is no rival to the reality. Even now, with my legs straddled across his waist, I still feel the hardness of him beneath me, making me wonder if he's always this rock solid, or if he's only taking a breather before plunging himself into me once more.

Whatever the outcome, I have no doubt I'll be one happy woman.

"What are you thinking about?" Kharon asks, twining his fingers through my hair.

I smile. "Us."

Turning to face me, Kharon smiles, pushing my hair out of my face. "I like hearing you say us. It makes me happy. You make me happy."

Sliding my hands through the length of him, I take him in my hand. "Yes, you both seem very happy."

His blonde hair hangs over his dark brows, and he plants a soft kiss on my cheek. "Can I show you how happy you make me?"

"I thought you already did?" I laugh.

Positioning himself on top of me, I gasp as I feel Kharon slide back into me. He wasn't joking. He *is* happy.

"I want to make love to you now, Rae," he whispers into my ear as he slowly rotates his hips, inching deeper into me with each thrust.

Moaning, I rake my hands along the muscles of his back, enjoying the steel of him inside me. "Didn't you do that already?"

Kharon groans in response, kissing my neck as his hands motion over my breasts as he circles his hips, grunting with each thrust. "Oh, that," he breathes into my neck. Looking at me between kisses, he smiles again. "Well, I think we both know that was something different."

His rhythm becomes more intense as he takes hold of my hands, clenching them above my head.

"What's the difference?" I whine beneath him.

Kharon shifts his weight back and forth, side to side, stretching me past what I thought I could take. Although we're laying on the ground, nestled in the softest silks and satins I've ever felt in my life, Kharon's movements make me feel like we're on a boat.

Hovering over me, Kharon pauses after planting himself deep, staring at me. "After all the years of pent-up passion, we both had a lot to get off our chests. I needed to be inside you so badly, I couldn't think straight."

His pause doesn't last long. As he rocks back and forth, my gasps turn into small screams as his pace quickens.

"And now?" I cry out as I watch the delight my bouncing breasts bring him as he rocks me to heights of ecstasy I never knew existed. He likes knowing what he's doing to me.

"Now, all I can think about is making you feel beautiful, loved, and pleased. Do I please you, Rae?"

"Yes, Kharon, yes!" I scream as I feel myself tighten and pulse around his length.

"Does it please you when I make you come?" Nodding in agreement, my body convulses as he continues pounding into me, holding my wrists captive, ensuring I feel everything he's giving me. "Then come for me, my little honeycomb."

At this rate, my poor vagina will be useless in the morning, and it's all thanks to Kharon Nyx.

With one final thrust, Kharon releases himself inside me again, panting hard as he leans into my neck, breathing me in.

"Us," Kharon groans as he kisses my cheek once more.

Fourteen

KHARON

With Rae's tight grip at my rear, it became evident she had no desire for me to slip out of her or out of my embrace. Still, being the bigger of the two of us, I insisted on flipping her over, straddling me so I wouldn't crush her under my weight.

I was more than pleased that Rae used the opportunity to ride me again. Our final, shared climax lulled her into a slumber so deep, I've done nothing but lay in awe of the beauty of Rae Vereen. From the curves of her perfect, evenly petite, five-foot frame rested on top of me to her long, sandy brown hair flowing like a tidal wave across my chest, I want nothing but to hold her like this forever.

It pains my heart more than she could possibly comprehend to know how my deception hurt her and her family. Even more, knowing that, despite my reasons, doing so kept me from holding the most perfect creature in my arms.

I'll never allow anything to come between us again.

As small fissures of light from the early morning sun weave through the shadows of my cave, I can't help admiring how each ray of light highlights just how beautiful Rae is. While I could hold her like this all day, I know her family will soon come looking for her.

Kissing the crown of her head, I gently squeeze her arm, hopeful to wake her. "Baby, it's time to get up," I say, running my hands through her lovely tendrils. Wiggling on top of me, grunting with the most adorable protest I've ever heard, Rae shakes her head, pushing her face into my chest. "I know, I didn't want to wake you either, but the sun is rising, baby."

"Umph," she pouts, turning her head away from me and leaning into my arm. "I like it right here," she whispers, gyrating against me, inviting me once more into her already wet center.

Once more, my manhood rises to the occasion, as my length easily slips inside her. "Baby, please," I grunt as she sits up, gliding herself atop me just as masterfully as she did last night. "We can't —" My words are garbled as I enjoy her rhythmic motion.

"Mm... we are," Rae whispers back as she takes my hands in hers, gliding me along her breasts as she continues her movements.

With her eyes closed, I almost wonder if she is indeed awake. If I didn't know better, I'd say she was dreaming. The thought alone intrigues me. If she is still sleeping, I can only hope she is dreaming of me. I wish I could tell her of all the nights I haunted her dreams. Hovering outside her window at night, I entered her dreamscape, only to find her dreaming of me.

At first, I rode along as a passenger in the night, relishing her passionate fantasies of us together. Over time, I participated, wholly taking part in her every desire. From her dreams of riding me, kneeling before me, or her legs hanging over my shoulders, I indulged her every whim. Only to watch from her window as she climaxed in the night to only her thoughts of me.

She isn't dreaming now.

"Yes, we are, beautiful," I groan in reply. Wrapping my arm tight around her waist, I push myself up against the cold stone wall so that I am almost face to face with her. I want her eye level with me when she hits her climax.

Draping her arms around my neck, Rae hums, relishing each thrust, tossing her head back in pleasure.

"Ahh...oh!" she screams as I begin to feel her walls tighten around me.

"Open your eyes, angel," I say with my mouth against hers. "I need you to look me in the eyes when I make you come."

Rae's eyes pop open, shocked. "Kharon?" she says, her eyes squinting as her breasts bounce against my chest as she cries out, her climax close.

Holding her hips down, I ensure she feels every thrust. "Yes, baby, I'm right here."

"Khar—baby!" she whines with her head tilted, back arched, perfect breasts on display.

I'm almost not prepared for my own release, but hearing her sweet nickname for me, I am suddenly overcome with a giddy feeling I've never experienced before.

"Give it to me!" I roar as I unload everything I have into her slick center. Give it to me she does as she bucks harder with each throb of her sweet center.

Slowly, we both relax from our climaxes as she leans into my hold, her head on my shoulder as I add a few final strokes while she whimpers into my embrace as she pulsates along my length.

A small chuckle escapes me as I shake my head, brushing her

hair away from her sweaty brow line. "So, you were dreaming?" I ask.

As she looks up at me with a wide, doe-eyed stare, my heart melts knowing this wonderful woman is far better than a monster like me deserves. Still, Rae smiles her usual shy smile, abandoning the desire-fueled woman who just rode me like her life depended on it.

Tears fill her eyes and my heart thumps, fearful she regrets all we've become to one another in such a short time.

I can't lose her.

A lone tear falls down her cheek, and I quickly wipe it from her face. The last thing I want to see in her eyes is sadness.

"Rae, please tell me what's wrong. Tell me what I can do to make it right." My words rush out as I feel her wiggle in my grip. I don't want to let her go, but I will not keep her against her will either.

"It's just—ugh!" She frowns as more tears run down her face. I cup her chin, intent to keep her focus on me.

I'm not sure if I'm prepared to hear what she has to say—especially if she's changed her mind about us—but I know better than to drag this out. "It's okay, Rae, just tell me."

"Well, you're right, Kharon. I was dreaming. In fact, I thought this was all a dream. I dreamt I came here to see you after the cotillion. In my dreams, you told me how you only did what you did to protect your sister. Then I dreamed you and I—that we..." Pausing, Rae looks up at me for a moment with a bashful glance, her cheeks blushing red.

"Made love?" I answer for her with a smile, tracing the outline of her luscious lips with my finger.

"I thought it was all a dream. Then I woke up, and we were doing everything I've dreamed about for years—I couldn't believe it was real—that this is real."

My throat clenches. "I need to confess something."

Rae's face scrunches some. "What is it?"

"I know about your dreams, Rae."

Her cheeks blush. "What do you mean?"

"All of those nights you dreamt of me–of us making love. I was there with you. It's called a haunting. My mother, Nyx, was a dreamwalker and so am I. It's not something I do often, or at all since I've been here. Only to you. I wanted–no I needed–to know if you were thinking of me like I thought of you."

Gasping, Rae covers her mouth. "So you know all of my dirty thoughts about you?"

Pulling her hand from her face, I plant a soft kiss on her lips, squeezing her butt and thrusting myself inside her tight little hole. "Did what I say frighten you? I hope you don't think I'm a monster."

Lifting up a bit, Rae slides back down on my shaft, rolling her hips until she hits her sweet spot. "Yes, but you're my monster. You can haunt my dreams anytime. Just mine," she moans into a kiss, swirling her hips around.

Fisting her hair, I lock our mouths together. "*Only you,*" I breathe into our kiss, as I continue fucking her until her eyes roll to the back of her head.

Fifteen

RAE

Gazing into Kharon's steely stare, my heart is overwhelmed with an influx of feelings. As he tugs me tighter into his hold, I realize I've never felt so free, safe, and loved before.

Never did I think our moment would ever really come to fruition.

Frankly, I thought he'd be the man of my dreams forever but never my reality. Yet here I am, my legs wrapped around his waist, hands hung over his back, staring into his eyes.

As messed up as everything is, I can say I've never been happier than I am right now.

Sure, my family doesn't know what I feel for Kharon and he for me, but in this moment, I could care less about who approves of what we have. I'm content staying in this position for the duration of my days...and nights.

"Only me, huh?" I smile, forcing away any impending clouds of doubt. Kharon's jaw tightens and his eyes narrow as he regards me. I know I'm not as subtle as I hoped.

"I'm sorry, Rae." Kharon's voice is heavy, and I can tell he's serious. I open my mouth to reply, but he doesn't give me an opportunity to protest. "I don't care if I have to apologize a thousand times -- please forgive my pursuit of Winter. I understand how much that hurt you, but letting you believe I wasn't interested in you surely hurts more."

Hearing Kharon's admission makes me want to cry. For as much as I wanted to fast forward past this pain, I know this is necessary. "It's okay, Kharon," I mutter, brushing my hair behind my ear, twirling my curls between my fingers, a very normal nervous response for me.

"No, Rae, it's not. I will not ask you to act like it is. While I know you understand my reasons, it doesn't change or take away the pain. For that, I am sorry. Please know I'll make it my life's pursuit from this moment forward to ensure you never feel like that ever again. On my soul I swear it if it be your will."

Holding my hand tight against his heart, the look in Kharon's eyes tells me I could end him with my next words, but I could never find a cause for ill toward his life. Ever. "I only want your soul and your heart to be happy. That is all I ever wanted. If I thought you'd have that with my cousin, I would want nothing but your happiness."

"Your beautiful heart is better than a wretch like me deserves, Rae Vereen. I promise you, I'll do all I can to make myself worthy of your loving and forgiving heart. I love you."

"I love you, Kharon," I cry, crushing my mouth to his. It's the best feeling in the world.

As he wraps his hulking arms around my tiny frame, the serenity I feel in his embrace is better than I could ever imagine. I always knew it could be like this for us, but nothing compares to this moment right now. How one who steers souls to Hades itself can make me feel like I'm in heaven, I'll never quite understand. All I know is I'll do whatever I must to ensure I feel like this forever.

Slowly releasing me from his hold and lifting my chin, he smiles. "So... Khar-baby?" he laughs.

Clasping my mouth with my hands, I realize I actually said my pet name for him out loud.

"It's okay. I love it," he laughs once more. "Although I must say, that one caught me by surprise."

"Oh, are you sure it doesn't sound juvenile? I mean, it's just something I always said when I—um, pretended my hands were yours at night."

Kharon's eyes darken immediately, and I feel his member flick hard against me again. "I like the thought of that. You did that every time?"

"All the time," I whisper, twirling my hair again.

A boyish smirk crosses his face, and I notice he looks even more youthful than before. "It's good to know we were thinking of each other at the same time."

"Oh, I'm sure we were in sync more than either of us can understand," I add, wiggling in his lap.

Shaking his head, his wavy blonde hair flies against his dark brows, illuminating his sexy contrast as his stormy eyes glare at me with desire. "Oh, no you don't, angel! I can't let you get us revved up again. The sun is rising, and you'll need to get back to your family soon. I'm sure they're worried." Kharon's eyes fall, and I know he doesn't want me to leave.

Taking his face in my hands, I lock in on his eyes. "You are my family now."

His eyes blossom like a dark flower at my admission, and I'm in awe at the vulnerability of this giant on whose lap I've become a fixture. Kharon is always so sure of himself, so strong; I can't help but feel fortunate he chose to share even an ounce of himself with me.

"And you are mine," he whispers, leaning his forehead against mine. "It is for that reason that I'll not allow anything to come in between you and the Elysians. I'm sure they're worried about you. While you may understand the truth, I won't give them another reason to despise me—at least, not before we have a chance to clear the air, but that will take some time."

Knowing that Kharon cares about how my family regards him —*regards us*--thickens the affection my heart holds for him. Just the thought sends a gushing stream straight to my core. Smiling as I feel him once more at my entrance, I know, despite his desire to ensure all is well between me and my family, his desire for me is stronger.

Right now, I plan on enjoying just how strong every part of Kharon Nyx can be.

Sixteen

KHARON

Once more watching Rae's butt jiggle as I smack it and pound into her, I know without a doubt that I am the luckiest man on the island, perhaps in both the Netherworld and this earthbound plane combined.

I don't know if it's because I've denied myself the joys of sensual pleasure since the day I came here—I thought such a pleasure could only be found in my heart's true love—but I never thought I could go on with as much vigor as I have with Rae. Knowing she has the fortitude to withstand and enjoy everything I am giving her makes me want to give it to her so much more.

In just our few short hours together, I've discovered Rae loves arching her back and displaying herself to me. I know she loves entrancing me with the bounce of her breasts as well as spreading her legs open, knowing I can't resist slipping into the prettiest little pearl my eyes have ever seen.

I wish I could say she doesn't know what she does to me, but the fact is, she is well aware, and she chooses every opportunity to tease me.

Honestly, if it were up to Rae, we'd spend the remainder of the day going at it.

One more thrust into her slick, wet opening, and we're both crying out as our shared climax hits its peak.

Grasping the thick blue fabric she wrapped around herself earlier, Rae collapses beneath me as her knees give way. I remain inside her, enjoying the feel of her pulsing core gripping me. She feels so damn good, I may never leave.

"Ahh, baby, if we keep this up, you'll never leave this cave, and you'll be my pretty little hostage for real," I whisper into her ear as she lays there panting, gripping the blue satin fabric at her side.

"It's all right, Kharon. I love being your pretty little hostage. Just promise to take care of me and never let me go," she moans, pressing her mouth to mine.

With a few more gentle strokes, I kiss her as I fill her with more of me. Gripping her hands above her head, the feel of my body pressed against hers comforts me in ways I never knew I needed.

Flipping her over, I kiss her again. "I'll never let you go, angel. You are all mine now, and I take care of what's mine. Now, let me take care of you."

And let me take care of her she does. I don't know the man I've become with Rae Vereen, but I am ravenous for her in ways that are indescribable.

Still, I promised to take care of her, and that is exactly what I do. Lifting Rae in my arms, I carry her to the back of my lowly dwelling, to a hidden hot spring nestled in the privacy of my hovel.

Gently washing her body, I do what I can to ensure the only trace of our time together is tucked away between her legs. While a mortal nose can't detect my Netherworld scent, I can't have the Guard roaming the island catch my scent on her. I'll not put her in a position to have to justify what we are to one another alone. When that time comes, we'll do it together.

Using one of my thicker fabrics to dry her off, my eyes can't help but linger on her sweet spot. As I stare at her sweet pink petals, opening like a dew-kissed flower just for me, I am instantly hard. I've never seen anyone as beautiful in the entirety of my long life.

"Baby, sit back," I say, tugging at her knees. Rae's smoldering stare makes my heart soar as her legs fall open, revealing the glory of her to my gaze. She knows what she's doing to me. "I've got to have the taste of your sweetness on my tongue."

All the nights I imagined what it would be like to taste her sweet center can't come close to the joy I feel with her in my mouth. Lapping at her like a thirsty man, I give attention to each nook and cranny. If cotton candy and strawberries had a baby, it would taste like Rae Vereen, the prettiest, sweetest thing I've ever known. It's so good, I know I'll never get enough.

"Good, sweet baby, that's it," I say as I wipe her arousal from my chin. I watch as she writhes, eyes closed, hands fisting the sheets. Slipping my finger into her opening, I rub the sensitive spot I know will make her see stars. "Let me take care of you," I add, lapping at her once more. "I'll always take care of you."

Grasping a handful of my hair in her hands, Rae moans, gyrating her hips as she climbed to her release. "I'll always give more than I take, Rae, but I promise to give more than you can possibly imagine."

Seventeen

RAE

I SHOULD BE ACCUSTOMED to Kharon's hands on my body, but after falling fast asleep after my last orgasm, I never imagined I'd find him as I do now, his rock-hard member aimed at me as he rubs a mixture of satin and silks all over my body.

"Khar?" I question, peering past the bright beams of sunlight entering the cave. Instantly twitching at his touch, I can't help but enjoy the feel of him exploring my body.

"Just lay still, baby," he smiles, running his hands along every part of me.

"What are you doing?"

Laughing, he smiles again. "Well, since my lady seems to fancy that blue fabric so much, I figured I'd give it to her. Since I destroyed the gown you wore earlier, I can't have you walking around naked."

"You can make clothes too?" I looked at him in shock.

"Oh, I have quite a few tricks up my sleeves," he adds, squeezing the fabric against my hips. "Now, be still." He winks at me, and I can't help admiring his youthful smile and bright eyes that look like they're dancing. Running his hands up my sides, he whispers an unknown tongue, and I feel the fabric cinch and tighten at my sides. "All done."

The broad smile and puffed chest give Kharon away. He's proud of his work.

Offering his hand, he helps me up from the floor and I look myself up and down, awestruck at the ensemble. A teal blue, wide-leg jumper sits masterfully on my frame, better fitting than anything I've ever purchased from a store.

"How is this possible?"

With another appreciative smirk, he picks up some gray fabric from the floor and tunics them around his waist. Quickly running his hands down his leg, a thick air of shock leaps from my throat as I watch the fabric transform into perfectly cut trousers.

"I'll give you the condensed version. I was raised by my aunt, Clotho. She kept a spinning wheel; she taught creatures of night to fashion fabrics from their bodily fluids. Sounds weird, I know—"

I looked at him in shock, my mouth agape. "Wait, you mean to tell me everything I learned of Greek and Roman deities was real?"

"I should hope so," he laughs, brushing his hands through his hair adding his panty-dropping smile. "I mean, mortals were taught mythologies. You know fragments of our history, but much of what you were taught as legend is very real. When my kind was relegated to the Netherworld, mortals were led to believe we were nothing more than myth and legend. They exchanged truth for lies, wrangling stories to suit their fancy. I happen to know Medusa is not a snake-haired, stone-inducing wench. She's actually a nice woman, a grandmother now, who likes baking bread."

My eyes grow wide in wonder. If Kharon wasn't who I know him to be, the *Ferryman of the Underworld*, I'd swear he was lying.

But he's not.

I'm so caught off guard by his admission, I hardly notice he's added more fabric to himself, making a shirt. Looking around the cavern, my eyes slowly fall as I watch Kharon tuck his shirt into his trousers.

"What's wrong, Rae?" he asks, taking my shoulders in his hands.

Shrugging a bit, I feel my cheeks warm, and I know I'm blushing. "Well, it's just, I thought I knew you—but now I feel like maybe I jumped the gun a little. I mean, I just had sex for the first time and I hardly know anything about you or where you come from."

Kharon's eyes fall at my admission. Turning his head over his shoulder quickly, he sighs at the sight of the rising sun before looking back at me. "Rae," he begins, taking my chin in his hands and lifting my head. "Last night was no mistake. It was the best part of my six hundred years."

"Six hundred?" I shriek. "You barely look a day over thirty."

"Well, more like twenty-five," he laughs, brushing his fingers through his hair.

I'm still looking at him incredulously. "How is that possible?"

"Things work differently in the Netherworld. Without the sun's influence, we don't age as fast. Time moves far slower. In mortal years, I've been around six hundred years, but where I'm from, I've barely lived. That's why when the Changelings cursed me with mortal-like aging, it sped me to death's door. It was your love, Rae, that reversed the curse."

My eyes went wide. "Okay, but what about—"

He interrupts me before I could continue. "I know you have

questions, and I promise to answer as many as I am able, but there's more pressing things we should tend to." Once more, Kharon's eyes dance, and I wonder how quickly my clothes will disappear this time.

Rising on my toes, I smile. "Like what?" I ask, twirling my hair between my fingers.

Lifting his arm above my head, he dangles a gathering of greenery. "A kiss. Merry Christmas!"

KHARON

DANGLING the mistletoe above where we stand, I wrap my free arm around her waist and pull her close. Locking our lips together, I feel a bolt of kinetic energy whip through me, as if another part of me is brought to life by the love of Rae Vereen.

Not only is this wonderful woman igniting a passion I thought long since lost, she makes me feel more alive than I've ever felt. I don't know if it's the softness of her lips or the sweetness of her luscious tongue as it swirls with mine, but I've never beheld such a precious gift on a Christmas morning.

And based on our endless lovemaking last night, Rae Vereen is indeed a gift that keeps giving.

As hard as it is, *and as hard as I feel myself becoming*, I pull away from our kiss. I know if we linger a minute longer, the lovely ensemble I created for Rae will undoubtedly unravel.

"Mmm... Merry Christmas, Kharon," she breathes, tugging my shirt, yanking me close to nab another kiss.

"Best holiday ever," I add, leaning my forehead against hers. "The first of many."

Rae pinches her chin between her fingers, scrunching her mouth in the cutest way. "Yeah, somebody said something about taking care of me for the rest of my life."

I smile. Sarcasm never sounded sweeter. "That somebody meant every word."

"Well, then why do I feel like I'm being kicked out? I mean, I know there's still more you have to share, but please don't tell me there's a Mrs. Kharon on her way back or something." Rae giggles but raises a cautious brow.

I know she's being cute, but just the insinuation frustrates me. "Rae." My voice deepens more than an octave. She jumps back a little, but I drop the mistletoe to the ground to grab her wrist. "Let me be perfectly clear. There has never been a Mrs. Kharon, but when that time comes, I assure you, you'll be the only woman with the title." Rae's eyes widen, and her mouth drops open in surprise. Taking her chin, I gently push her jaw to close her mouth. "But if you prefer that I be called Mr. Rae, I am more than open to the notion. I am a feminist, after all." I smile, hopeful she knows how serious I am.

"Wow, Kharon," Rae begins, her eyes watering. "You have no idea how long I've wanted to hear you say those words. I know I have more to learn, but I doubt there's anything you can say to change how I feel, how I've always felt about you. I love you."

Kissing her cheek, I run my hand through her pillowy soft hair. "And I love you, Rae Vereen."

"To the moon and back?" she laughs, solidifying her hold on my back.

"How about to Pluto's moon?"

Tilting her head, curious, Rae chuckles. "Pluto?"

"Not up on your astronomy, huh? Well, I suppose my moon was discovered forty years ago, so that is a bit beyond you."

"While I'd like to know how you got a moon named after you, I want to get back to you being six hundred years old." Stepping back, I narrow my gaze. I'm pretty sure I know where this is going. "You say you're six hundred or so, but I know the legend of the Ferryman has been around a lot longer."

"The easiest way to explain it is that I was born into the order of Ferrymen. My father, Erebus, owed a debt to a powerful Changeling witch. When he didn't pay his due, he promised the lives of his children. To protect us, my mother, Nyx, divided us, the *Kharon*, the Ferrymen, between the Styx and Acheron Rivers, binding us there in servitude, cloaking us from the Changeling until we reached maturity. We serve at their behest until we die. I am the last one."

Gasping, Rae covers her mouth with her petite hands. Thick, glassy tears fill her eyes, and for the first time, she regards me with the one thing I never hoped to see: pity.

"I am so sorry, Kharon!" Rae says, clasping her hands at her chin. "Please forgive me for pushing." Reaching for my hand, Rae tries to smile to cover the sadness marring her perfect face, and it makes me smile in return.

Surprisingly, I don't feel pitied. It's quite the opposite. In my entire life, I have never received such benevolence. Not only has she completely forgiven my trespasses, but she still manages to have a modicum of empathy for my plight.

"There's nothing to forgive, beautiful. You asked a question, and I gave an answer. I promise you, as long as I live, I shall always answer you truthfully. I cannot promise you the things I have to share will always be easy to accept or understand, but I promise you the truth. Always."

"Always," she repeats in a whisper, leaning her head to my chest.

Kissing the crown of her head, I firm my hold around her. "Just promise me one thing."

"Anything," Rae says, looking up at me with the earnest stare that melts my heart.

"Promise me, despite how hard things may get from here, we're in this together. Always."

"Together. *Always.* I like the sound of that."

"So do I, beautiful."

Nineteen

RAE

Crushing his mouth to mine, Kharon's lips caress mine with a care I never knew I needed. Moving his mouth in a rhythmic motion so gentle yet commanding it's like he's steering a ship. Like water, his tongue glides effortlessly around my own, taming it into willful submission, and I am all too eager to reverently bow to his will.

I pant like an overindulgent child, her popsicle taken away, when he pulls his mouth from mine. I want *more*.

"It's Christmas morning. Your family will be looking for you. The last thing we need is to raise suspicion, at least not until we get matters straight with your family." Kharon's thumb traces the outline of my lips as he leans his forehead to mine. "Believe me when I tell you, letting you go right now is harder than you could ever imagine."

Sighing, I stifle my urge to kiss him yet again, knowing it will be that much harder to pull away a second time. "It's tough for me, too, and it's also Win's birthday. I've never missed it."

"Well, we shouldn't dally. I'll take you there myself."

Stepping back, I'm surprised at Kharon's suggestion. "I thought you were trying to keep a low profile."

"That's what the onyx sand is for." He smiles, walking to the stone table and retrieving the velvet box he showed me last night. "Besides, with coyotes and bears around, I hardly feel comfortable letting you go without me. It's not safe."

Kharon casts a cagey smile, but his eyes bounce around the cave a bit before landing back on mine. This isn't the first time I've seen him avert his gaze. Usually, he seems to do so in the hopes I don't notice him watching me, but this time feels different.

"What is it, Kharon?" I ask, worried. "This seems to be about more than coyotes and bears."

Shrugging his shoulder, Kharon tucks the velvet box inside his pocket and swipes his hair from his face. All my life, twisting my fingers through my curly hair has been my go-to when I'm nervous. While I know Kharon is strong enough to face anything on his own, there's a new vulnerability to him now that's all too familiar.

"Please, Kharon, you can tell me. The truth, remember?" Circling where he stands, my eyes plead with him.

He sighs. "I need to go look for my obol. I'm sure Lux still has it, and I need to reclaim it from him. It's not safe for me to be apart from it for long."

Panic bubbles within me as Kharon's disquieting disposition troubles me, just as it did last night. While I'm sure the kiss Winter shared with Lux to unbreak Melchior's prison seemed like something out of a fairytale, for me, it was the most heart wrenching moment of my life. Seeing how grief-stricken Kharon became and knowing the pain he endured tortures my heart.

"Tell me what's going on." Gritting my words through my teeth is neither sexy nor alluring, but right now, I don't care. Seducing the man I love is the last thing on my mind right now.

Taking my shoulder in his hand, Kharon forces a smile while using his other to brush away a few loose strands of hair from my face. "I don't want you to worry, but you should know it's not safe for anyone while my obol is gone. The last time I was separated from it, your cousin found it. That's how the Changelings were able to conjure their prism to keep him hostage."

"Okay," I begin, my eyes searching Kharon's face. I'm troubled to still see caution in his eyes. "And?" I question, demanding he tells me the whole story. "Spit it out, Kharon. I can take it. We're in this together, remember?"

"Together," he breathes, blowing his wispy blonde tendrils away from his forehead. "It's Moirai, Rae. I need to recover the obol to save my sister."

I gulp. "And by saving her you mean returning to the Netherworld?"

"Yes." Kharon's answer is like a punch to my gut.

The Netherworld is the last place I want him to go. It's the place that imprisoned my cousin for over a decade. It's the place holding Moirai hostage now, and it's the place he must return to, leaving me here, alone.

This is the ski lift all over again. We've only just begun, and we must be separated again. Swallowing the tight air nearly choking my next words, I force my selfish thoughts aside. "What do you need me to do?" I ask, lifting my chin, defying my own heart's cry to beg him to stay.

Kharon's chest swells with pride, admiration sweeping a smile across his face. "How a monster like me is permitted such a grace from your beautiful heart, I'll never understand. I will work a thousand lifetimes to make myself worthy of such a rare and perfect gift. With all that I am, I love you, Rae Vereen."

Once more, Kharon lifts my chin, kissing me as though it was the last time. My salty tears mesh between us, but Kharon holds firm at the nape of my neck, locking our mouths together.

For this moment, it's all I need.

Deepening our kiss, I wrap my arms around his waist. Taking this moment to enjoy the rippling muscles of his physique, it's all I can do to force away the looming heartache that inevitability awaits me.

For now, being in the arms of the monster who loves me is all I could ever want.

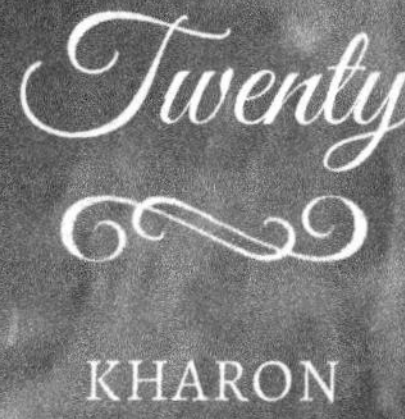

Twenty

KHARON

HOLDING Rae in my arms is a sacred duty I'll cherish forever. Yet, unlike sweeping her away from beasts in the cold of night, I nestle this beautiful breaker of curses in my arms, clinging to her for dear life.

Rae Vereen has revived the walking corpse I once was, and only Rae Vereen can end it. How I've been afforded such love, I'll never understand, but holding her like this reminds me that everything I've ever wanted is right here, in my arms.

Gliding effortlessly through the snow-capped forest, we make our way to the edge of Elysian Manor. If it weren't Christmas morning and if I didn't know her family would be expecting her, I would have taken my time, showcasing my Nether-magic and skill. Instead, Rae only got to see me sprinkling onyx sand and my ability of flight. Although she got an impromptu display of my ability to fly last night, I always imagined giving her a more eloquent first look, befitting the woman I love.

Thankfully, she seems just as amazed. Her eyes are full of wonder as she nestles into my chest. Taking in the view of deer traipsing through the snow and the small flock of birds flying at our side, Rae marvels at the simple grandeur of it all.

Arriving just outside the warming post near the stables, I gently land us at the gates. A few horses stir a bit, startled by our arrival, but I speak the sacred words of *peace* in Nether tongue to ease their angst.

"They can understand you?" Rae asks, surprised.

"Yes," I smile, peering out from under my trench coat. "Animals were here when our worlds were one and the same. Those that remain understand our words."

"Even Mr. Puddles?" Rae giggles. "I'm sure that'll ruffle Win's feathers. She thinks she's the only person who understands her prized French Canadian."

My eyes continue searching around the stables, ensuring we're alone. "Who do you think your uncle asked to tame Mr. Puddles?" That's not all I've done for her uncle over the years, but I'll save that for another time.

"I should've known," she smirks, adding a kiss to my chin as I look around.

"Okay, beautiful, this is where we part. When I release you, you'll be visible again, so you'll have to continue on without me."

She looks up at me with hope. "Maybe I can help you find the obol?"

"No, Rae!" I lash my words as hard as I can, but I force a smile so as not to frighten her. "Please promise you'll never touch that stone. If you find it, just wait for me. Do not touch it. If the Changelings were to do anything to you, I—"

Placing her small pointer finger on my lips, Rae smiles, looking up at me through her thick lashes. "Shush," she starts, adding a doting smile. "I'm not going to do anything to endanger myself, I promise."

I sigh. "Thank you."

"Besides, I think you'd have a harder time getting a kiss from my brother to free me." She laughs and I want to laugh with her, but the thought is unnerving. Just thinking of those wretched witches issuing a curse upon her life is too awful to fathom.

Still, looking at her now, I can't help smiling. "How do you do that?"

"Do what?"

"Make me smile when everything inside me says I'm at the end of my rope."

"Well, Mr. Nyx, I suggest you tie a knot and hold on tight, because I have it on good authority that I pull good string." Gliding her tongue along her gleaming white teeth, Rae's passionate prowess is on full display.

With a wink, Rae blows me a kiss, slipping out from under my hold. As she steps back, her eyes grow wide, shocked by my invisibility. Even though she can't see me, she smiles and offers a small wave.

"I'll meet you back here at sunset," Rae whispers as her eyes gaze around the stable.

I thrash the heel of my boot into a muddy puddle, catching her attention. She smiles again, biting her lip in the most adorable way before turning quickly toward the manor.

Watching her leave is both painful and pleasurable. It hurts knowing we're apart, but there's a new, confident bounce in her stride this morning. Knowing I'm responsible for this new sway of her perfectly round ass invigorates parts of me I can't wait to share with her again.

And again…

Twenty-One

RAE

I'm GRINNING like a giddy fool, I know, but neither the whipping wintry wind as I stand at the back door nor the eminence of what will ensue once I tell my family about me and Kharon can wipe this ridiculous grin from my face.

I am in love.

Not only did I spend the night making love to the man of my dreams, but I am totally at a loss for words, knowing all we've become to one another in such a short time. Over the years, I could only hope this day would come. Now that it's here, my life will never be the same.

As much as I wish telling my family would not be an uphill

battle, I am confident whatever we have to face next, Kharon and I can and will do it together.

Yes, together. I love the sound of that.

"Where in the blazes have you been?" I'm quickly pulled from my musing when I feel Ross' tight hold on my arm, yanking me into the kitchen. "Out with it, missy!" Ross snaps as he looks me over.

"Good morning to you, too, brother," I reply, tearing away from his grasp.

"Oh, don't be coy with me, sister!" he bites back.

"Merry Christmas." I dance around him, twirling to avoid his eyes as I make my way to the fridge.

Forcing the door closed before I have a chance to grab the pitcher of juice, Ross leans his lanky frame in to meet my eyes. I've never been able to keep a secret from Ross. Ever. I know it'll only take one look for him to discover the truth behind my glee.

Narrowing his sharpened stare, my brother searches my face. Dragging his gaze along the entirety of me, his eyes nearly pop from their sockets as his mouth drops open in a gasp.

"You little strumpet!" he jeers, jabbing his long, pointy finger into my shoulder. "Who? What? When? *Where?*" Ross nearly chokes out the last word as he shakes my shoulders.

"Mmm... did someone say crumpets?" Our uncle's merry voice echoes through the hallway. "I hope there's still honey and gooseberry jam left. That is, if Ross hasn't eaten it all!" Uncle El calls.

"Honestly, I don't know where Ross stores it all," Aunt Vivian adds as she and Uncle El make their way into the kitchen. "If I take one nibble, I have to do thirty planks just to burn it off." Chuckling like a schoolgirl, my aunt's smile is bright as she comes into view. Although she's normally a tad stoic and brusque, Christmas morning has always been joyful for her. I suppose giving birth to her only child is reason enough to celebrate, but having Melchior back home must make today better than most.

Ross shoves my shoulder, shooting me a playfully condemning glare before pushing away from the fridge.

"Yes, there are plenty strumpets," he hisses beneath a cupped hand. "I mean, crumpets left, Uncle El." Winking at me as he grabs a jar of honey from the shelf, he places it on the table for them.

"Um, where is Win?" I ask, really wondering where Lux is. Although I have no intention of touching the obol as Kharon insisted, putting my sights on it means Kharon can save his sister. No one answers me. Typical. They simply carry on as they always do, ignoring me.

"Merry Christmas, everyone!" Melchior cheerfully announces as he comes in from the side door.

"Merry Christmas, son!" Uncle El exclaims, quickly rising from his chair to hug his son.

"Melchior, dear, please don't tell me you've been outside without a coat," Aunt Vivian chides as he kisses the top of her head. "Why are you limping? Are you okay?"

"Oh, Vivian, don't make a fuss. He's a grown man," Uncle El says, as he sits back down. Grabbing a butter knife, he begins spreading honey on his crumpet.

"Thank you, Father," Melchior answers with a strained smile, making his way to the coffee pot.

"Women will try to mother you to your grave if you let them," he playfully grumbles, tossing a heap of bacon on his plate.

Swiping his hand and taking away three strips of bacon from him, Aunt Vivian shakes her head. "Yes, and without us women, you men would eat your way to an early grave. You complain about us, but you need us."

I smile as my mind drifts to Kharon. I can only hope he finds the obol soon. The sooner he finds it, the faster we can get back to *us*. Besides, I'm sure I could disappear again without much notice.

Ross taunts me from across the room with his arms folded

across his chest. *"I'm watching you,"* he mouths, pointing two fingers from his eyes towards me.

Thankfully, no one see his machinations as they continue eating breakfast. As odd as it is, I'm used to being unnoticed. It's not blatant disregard, but they certainly don't take me seriously. However, Melchior steps between me and Ross, shifting a mildly probing stare over his shoulder. Hunching his shoulders, he steps closer to the table as he sips his coffee.

"Well, actually, I thought everyone was joining us outside," Melchior says.

"Us?" I wonder.

"Yes. Lux is teaching Win to ice skate. She's actually taking to it quite well after falling on her bum a time or two." Melchior laughs, setting his cup down on the table. "So, who's joining us?"

Hopeful to get out from under my twin's daggered-eyed stare, I lift my hand. "Me!"

Twenty-Two

KHARON

I'm surprised how quiet the grounds of Elysian Manor are this morning. While Elysian gives his staff time off until after Boxing Day, I expected there to be a full-on search for me. There's no trace of the Guard nor any of Elysian's security detailing the property.

Although it helps me get around without much concern, I am slightly disappointed. For the last few years, I've spent my days as a trusted friend to Elysian. In that time, I've stressed how important it is for him to ramp up security, specifically around his estate. He's taken most of my advice to heart, beefing up security where needed, yet in one night, it's like he's disregarded all my advice.

But why? Why would he so flagrantly ignore all I've taught

him? Especially when the one he believes his primary adversary has yet to be captured. I can only wonder what lies the Guard has fed him to cause him to act so foolishly.

Still, I cannot linger on the issue. I need to find my obol.

I sense its power is still on the island, but for some reason, the exact location escapes me. Perhaps I've been on this earthbound plane for so long, I've lost some of my Nether-like sensibilities. The same way Lux and his brother were able to pry the obol from right under me, I am at a loss for its location now.

Remaining unseen as I sweep through the mansion, I make my way upstairs and find Rae's bedroom. It's the first time I've been on this level, but the scent of her carried me right to her suite, situated next to her cousin's room.

While I don't go into Winter's room, I'm impressed by Rae's décor. Unlike the neutral palette of the estate, Rae's room is vibrant and full of color. Bright shades of yellow, orange, blue and green perfectly mirror her vibrance. Rae has always been the bright, bubbly, albeit more bashful, one of the Elysian family. Whether she's trading inside jokes with her twin or bouncing around the kitchen while baking all sorts of decadence, I've long known there remained a hidden treasure in Rae.

I'm simply thankful to have unearthed such a treasure. My manhood flinches at the thought.

Looking around her room, I see a large book on her desk, *Rae's Recipe's* scrolled across the cover, I figure it's not too intrusive for me to sneak a peek. Recipes for muffins, cupcakes, and cakes are the first I see, and it warms my heart at just how much she enjoys baking. It's when I see the scribbling of *Khar's Scones*, though, my interest piques.

Recalling the day she brought orange and cranberry scones by her uncle's office for his birthday, my heart flutters. Elysian was grumbling with his secretary, barely a lick of gratitude for his niece's kind gesture, when she offered me a scone. With the way she perched the basket near her bosom, it didn't take much persuasion for me to take a bite. It was by far the best thing I ever tasted. Scones usually taste like day old bread to me, but hers was sweet and moist, just like her.

I told her she should make more and sell them at the next festival, to which she blushed. Seeing how she named them after me reassures me that my opinion matters to her.

Trailing my hand along her bedspread, my thoughts return to the intimacy we shared last night. Memories of her beautiful body laid before me go straight to my groin, and I wish she were in my arms. Heaving in copious amounts of her scent as I lift a pale blue satin chemise from her side chair near the window, I whisper *I love you* in Nether tongue as my thoughts linger on last night.

The sweet, dulcet sound of Rae laughing turns my attention to the window. Gazing through the blinds, the sight of her lovely face as she skates, holding her cousin's hand, makes me smile. All I want is to see the sun shining on her face, her world happy. I know it will take more than an apology before her family accepts all we've become to one another, but I will do all I can to earn their forgiveness and trust.

For a moment, I'm happy watching Rae and the Elysian family, but when I see Lux and a few other supernaturals come into view, a tinge of anger gnaws at me, along with something else. Jealousy.

I spent years inserting myself into the Elysian family and becoming a trusted ally. To see all I worked so hard for so easily substituted by that hybrid wolf enrages me to new heights. It's not that I envy his pairing with Winter, but it's time I set things right.

Twenty-Three

RAE

"You look beautiful, Rae," Aunt Vivian says, offering us hot chocolate. "Is that a new outfit?"

"It *is* lovely," Ross adds, skating up to me from behind. He shoots me a look, but I brush him off.

"Aww, did you get it for Rae for Christmas?" Winter asks, smiling broad as Lux walks toward us. "I mean it looks like it was made for you."

"Oh, yes it sure fits like a glove!" Ross snips over his shoulder, shooting me a cagey grin.

"Well, I bet you can't wait to take off that coat so you can show it off!" Winter gleams.

Gently bumping into my shoulder, Ross raises a brow. "You need to keep it on."

"Enough about me." I push by Ross, skating closer to the bench where my aunt sits. "How's the birthday girl? And the happy couple?" I force a wide smile as I watch the dreamy-eyed stare my cousin gives her fiancé.

She beams bright. "I'm good! I mean, *we* are good!" Winter locks her arm tight with Lux's as they share a laugh.

Lux offers a gracious smile in return, but all I can think about is where he's hiding Kharon's obol. His pants are fitted, so much so they seem to keep no secrets. I flit my eyes around a bit, hopeful no one sees me giving my cousin's beau a once over. If that wasn't bad enough, I seemed to be the odd one out, pining over Kharon as he pursued my cousin, and I certainly don't want to appear like I'm doing the same to Lux. I'm sure anyone would find Lux's creamy brown skin, dark wavy hair, and tight body an impeccable find, but he is no Kharon Nyx.

My Kharon.

"How are you doing, Rae?" Winter asks, her tender eyes searching mine. "I know everything was just too much for you last night and that's why you left. I wanted to check on you, but Ross insisted we give you some space."

Ross glares at me over Winter's shoulder. Twisting his mouth, he shoots me a knowing glance that I hope no one else sees.

"I'm fine," I force out. I really don't want anyone making a fuss over me. "I just needed a little space, like Ross said." I try to lift my mouth into a smile, but with everyone watching me, my attempts falter. "But it's Christmas, and your birthday! No reason to dally on the negatives," I add, taking a sip of my cocoa.

"Rae is right," Aunt Vivian chimes in, taking my hand and giving it a squeeze. "I'm going to take my old lady bones inside before I freeze. Win, darling, enjoy your lesson. I need to find your father. Something tells me he's wandered back into the kitchen for more bacon."

Shaking her head as she walks away, she stops to talk to Melchior, holding himself up against the fence.

"What's wrong with Melchior?" I ask, standing from my seat. Everyone turns to look, and I'm thankful to avert the attention from myself.

"Your cousin said his knee gave out," Stephen, Ross's new plaything, says, joining our huddle. My brother's face brightens as he studies his favorite lumberjack. "I think your aunt told him not to push himself too hard."

"Well, you just push your handsome self right to my side, boyfriend," Ross coos, extending his arms wide for Stephen. The two share a quick kiss before Ross leans back, examining Stephen like he just struck gold. "Look at you, looking all lovely. I've never seen anything nicer on ice."

Stephen blushes beneath his thick beard, shrugging his shoulders awkwardly. "Good morning, everyone!" He waves. Ross, however, keeps his arms wrapped tight around Stephen's waist, grinning like the same giddy fool he accused me of being.

As we belt a greeting in unison, I can't help being happy for my brother. He's spent so much time being a playboy, and he seems to have found something more in Stephen. While I'm hardly one to believe in the impossible these days, Stephen might actually be the one to make my twin settle down.

"I'm sure Big Mel will be just fine," Ross says, returning attention to our cousin. "I mean, he just got back from Dante's Inferno. I think he could use a breather."

Winter casts a puzzled stare. "Dante's Inferno?"

"You know, just another word for hell," Lux whispers.

Winter's brows raise in response, but then crease into a frown. "Well, it's a good thing Kharon Nyx evaporated into nothingness!

After everything he put my brother through, hell is too good for him!"

My cheeks warm at Winter's outburst, but I do my best to keep my anger in check. While I'm relieved everyone believes Kharon merely faded from existence, I am thankful it's not true.

"Is that what happened to him?" I play dumb. "Did his medallion thingy vanish too?" I sound even dumber, but it's best to keep the pretense.

"Well, no," Lux answers quickly. "We're keeping it safe in your uncle's vault until we can find a way to destroy it. My brother has an old friend visiting soon who may be able to help. That way, we'll be done with all things Kharon Nyx, once and for all."

"And good riddance!" Ross chimes in, and he and Winter high-five each other.

Fear tumbles through me at the thought that perhaps Kharon will be unable to free Moirai. As much as I wish to keep him here, with me, I want him to save his sister. I don't have time to let panic have its way with me when a small fluttering of birds rushes from the trees nearby and a branch breaks, falling onto the ice. No one else seems to notice, but I do.

A wispy breeze wafts a hint of smoke by my nose, and I smile. Even though I can't see him, I know he's nearby, which means he heard everything.

Twenty-Four

KHARON

Bonnie and Clyde. Who knew?

I have to say, I am more than impressed at how well Rae and I work together. No sooner did I make my way outside did she find a way to inquire about the obol. It's like she knew I was there. That warms all parts of my wretched soul.

Learning Elysian has it in his vault is exactly what I need to know. As hard as it is for me to take my eyes off Rae, I have to for now. Once I have the obol, I can save my sister from the captivity of the Changelings. Only then will I truly be able to start my life with Rae—our new life. Together.

Making my way inside Elysian's office chamber, I am thankful to find it empty. The faint stench of Altrinion vampires and wolves remains from their visit with Elysian last night, but I forge onward toward his vault.

My enhanced vision allows me to see the imprint of Lord Elysian's fingerprints along the keypad. Focusing on the deepest imprint first, I try a series of numbers until the vault unlocks. I'm not surprised he used Melchior's birthday. I frown; he never put my advice into practice.

Still, I don't take time to worry about it when I see my obol, gleaming like a diamond inside an almost empty chamber. Nothing but a strangely familiar golden urn sits inside. For a moment, I wonder if it's the remains of his late wife, Melchior's mother. Though I distinctly recall seeing her urn in the family crypt, I force the thought aside.

Nothing matters but getting my obol, saving my sister, and returning to Rae in one piece.

Reaching inside, I quickly grab my obol and sigh as I feel its power rivet through my body. Shaking off my trench and tearing myself free of my shirt, I feel like an inferno is brewing within me. Shimmering embers, like small flames of fire, implode through my pores and I feel a new strength overtake me. It's almost as reinvigorating as when Rae unlocked the Changeling's curse with her kiss, the full force of Nether magic sending rippling kinetic energy through me.

Letting out a low growl, I feel my muscles contort, bulging out from under my sleek, boyish frame. Like I'm a gym rat, fueled by protein, and bench pressing in my sleep, my biceps bulk and my pectorals expand. Every part of me seems to enlarge, and I can only hope *every part* of me pleases Rae.

Threading my obol through a leather cord, I quickly work it around my neck. This time, I chant the words to bind the obol to me. No one will ever steal it from me again, not even the Changelings. Only when I was separated from it were they able to curse me, and I won't let that happen again.

Gusts of steam erupt from my back as the flames subside, melting into my volcano-like skin. Letting out a heavy sigh, I stretch my arms, cracking my knuckles as I turn around. It's been too long since I've felt like myself. *Welcome back*, I smile.

"What did I tell you, Lord Elysian? I knew he'd come, like a moth to a flame."

Opening my eyes to find the leader of the Guard, Dalcour Marchand, standing with Elysian and a few others, my anger explodes. He's the bloody Altrinion vampire who made it his business to expose my secrets to Winter's fiancé and family. I hardly blame Lux for wanting to protect Winter. His motives are admirable. Dalcour, however, has far less commendable intentions.

"Did you really think it would be that easy?" Dalcour scoffs as he paces between the darkened corners of the room. I notice the oak shutters are drawn tight, and I see a dark cloth covering the transom.

Damn vampires. Leave it to them to block the sun. Piss me off enough, and the sun will be the last thing they see.

"Did you think I'd let you waltz around my property unchecked, Nyx?" Elysian lashes at me, but I keep my gaze fixed on Dalcour and the small brood surrounding him. "I have no idea how you rid yourself of your ghastly nature, but I am not fooled! You may look like a new man, Nyx, but Lord Marchand assured me you'd be up to no good. He prepared me well."

I rolled my eyes. "Yes, Lord Elysian, but I was the one who prepared you for times like this. Have I not advised you to strengthen your security?"

Throwing up his hand, Elysian swipes it through the air. "For all I know, you did it to keep me ignorant of your heinous deeds."

Before I have a moment to protest, Dalcour steps closer to Elysian's side. "Of that, I have no doubt, my friend." His placating tone annoys me, but it's the haughty smirk beneath his thick goatee that enrages me to new heights. Still, I work hard to maintain my angst. Elysian is Rae's family. Whether he understands it or not, I do care for them. "Now we have him."

Dalcour Marchand, though, has earned my hate.

I grunt. "Have me?" Grabbing my trench from the ground, I hang it over my arm. "Oh, I assure you, you don't have what you think. Your biggest mistake was allowing me to retrieve my obol. If your vampire confidant knew anything of worth, he'd know that was his first mistake," I say to Elysian.

"Are you so certain?" Dalcour answers darkly, rubbing his gloved hands together. "I have it on good authority that there are more important things than your worthless stone."

My eyes narrow as I sense movement on the other side of the room. Lux's brother and a woman I saw with him last night step out from the shadows, holding a large duffle. For a minute, I worry for Rae's safety, but I know Elysian would never put a member of his family in danger.

My heart nearly sinks when I see Lux's brother and the woman pull Moirai's stone from the bag. *No.* It can't be.

Stepping toward me, Dalcour's crimson eyes glow as he casts a cagey grin. "It's like I said, Ferryman, more important things."

Twenty-Five

RAE

My nerves are a wreck. We've skated around the lake more times than I can count, and each time, I look toward my uncle's office. I haven't seen anyone go in that direction, and part of me says that's a good thing. With Kharon maintaining his invisibility, no one should be able to see him.

I can only hope he's found his obol and is making plans to retrieve his sister.

As annoying as my brother is, I can't imagine anything happening to him. I love him with all that I am. Even now, as I watch him and Stephen skate hand-in-hand like lovebirds, my heart flutters knowing he's happy. While Stephen is a man of few words, he seems to be enough for Ross. Insisting my brother take classes in hospitality management, he's been instrumental in gearing Ross up for one day taking a bigger part in the operations of the bed and breakfast.

Truly, Ross is my uncle's best bet. Winter only dreams of opening her own school for supernatural children. Who knows whether Melchior will return to his Indiana Jones-like antics, looking for rare artifacts? As for me, if I could ever get my plans to open a bakery off the ground, I'd gladly help with the breakfast side of things. We're probably my uncle's only hope for his legacy.

As happy as I am watching them, I once again feel like the odd one out. I kept up with Ross and Stephen as much as I could, but while I was glancing at Uncle El's office, my pace slowed, and they went ahead.

"I'll be right there," Stephen shouts to his brother Sam, who calls to him from near the wooded lot. Sam runs the lumber mill nearby, and my uncle contracts out Christmas pine work to him. Although they're all part of the human nobles in the Regency, Sam prefers to stay away from supernaturals altogether. It's no wonder he stands on the other side of the fence, refusing to come close. By the bewildered look on his face, he's rather wary of Lux and the other wolves.

I wish he knew he had nothing to fear. Lux seems rather chipper and fun, which is exactly what my cousin needs. Oddly enough, I'm sure the same stare he's giving Winter and Lux is the same one I'll get when my family discovers I'm in love with the Ferryman of the Netherworld. All I can hope is for them to one day see Kharon for who he truly is, not the monster they think him to be.

"Hey you!" Ross surprises me, rushing to my side. "Why are you all misty-eyed?" Taking my hand, Ross leads us back to the side bench. After he helps me to my seat, he huffs and plops down beside me. "Okay, Pippin," he smiles, tapping the bridge of my nose. "Tell Merry all about it."

As I untie my skates, I can't help laughing. Memories of me, Ross, and Win playing dress up with Aunt Vivian's clothes run through my mind. Uncle El gave us nicknames when our aunt went all Gollum on us after we dropped her ring down a vent. Of course, he named Winter Arwen, but Ross and I affectionately became Merry and Pippin. All these years later, I guess it stuck.

Running a hand through my hair, I exhale hard. I haven't a clue where to begin. Folding one leg over the other, I palm my face. My nerves are a mess! All I can do is crack a faint smile while leaning my chin on my wrist.

"Wow!" Ross gasps. "This mystery man--I assume it is a man —" I nod, blinking twice for yes. "Well, whoever *he* is clearly has you at a loss for words. I need to find and thank him. My little chatterbox of a sister is actually quiet."

"Little?" I sit up, crossing my arms and feigning a frown. "You may be tallest, but I was born more than a whole ten minutes before your stubborn ass made an appearance."

Leaning his forehead to mine, he smiles. "You know me, I love to make an entrance. Tell me this: whoever he is, was he kind? Did he treat you like the queen you are?" Ross lifts a cautious brow, awaiting my answer.

"Better." The word rushes out like a gust of wind, hitting Ross smack in the face.

"Well damn, Curly Sue! Somebody got their world officially rocked to near heaven!"

Tossing my head back, I laugh. The same giddy feeling from before takes over. "Oh, it was heaven. And it was hell. But then, Ross, then—it was bliss!"

My brother's hazel eyes nearly pop out of his sockets. The faint freckles of his caramel-coated skin form a perfect figure eight around his nose as his mouth drops open. "Okay, I need details!

Who is this man? Tell me now." Ross squeezes my knee and I sit up, ready to spill it all.

"Well, it looks like the lovebirds are leaving us," Stephen says from behind us. Ross and I look up, surprised to see Winter and Lux heading toward the cabin near the lumberyard. "Didn't you hear them say they were leaving? Lux said he had a surprise for her. Sam came to tell me they cleared the cabin for them. He's still so scared of supernaturals, but I don't know why. I told him Lux was cool."

For the first time since I've seen Ross and Stephen together, Ross pays his beau no mind. Instead, he keeps his pointed gaze aimed at me.

"Oh, okay," Stephen continues as his gaze shifts between us. "Did I just walk up on some twin thing?"

Blushing, I bite my lip and look away from my brother. I'm not sure I'm ready to divulge all the details.

"I'm waiting, missy," Ross says, giving me his no-nonsense stare.

A whirlwind of thoughts zip through my mind as I struggle with the best way to tell Ross about Kharon. Twirling my fingers through my curls, my mind journeys back to the ski lift. Maybe I should start at the beginning? Before I can part my lips, though, the sound of raised voices near my uncle's office draws my attention.

This can't be good.

Twenty-Six

KHARON

"LORD ELYSIAN," I begin, my voice trembling. I keep my eyes on Moirai's stone but dart a cautious glance between Elysian and Dalcour. "Please, I implore you, if you ever felt an ounce of kinship with me, do not do anything rash."

"Do not speak to me of kinship, my boy!" he snaps. "You stand here, in my chamber, a changed man. Not even a semblance of the grotesque thing I saw of you last night remains. How? I do not know. All I know is because of you, I thought my son dead. Because of you, I missed time that cannot be replaced. So, do not speak to me of kinship. My kin—my son--laid in repose at your hand! Even now, you offer no apology, but you stand in my very presence bartering for a wretched stone!"

"Steady yourself, my lord," Dalcour adds, patting Elysian's shoulder. "Not only am I certain Changeling witchery is responsible for his new appearance, but I'd wager this stone has something to do with it."

"Once again, your arrogance proceeds you," I grumble. It's taking all my willpower to restrain myself. I don't want to do anything reckless that could endanger my sister, but I swear, if they break her stone, I shall release a fury the likes of which they've never seen. "Whatever you think you know of Changelings is but a fraction of how dire things can become if you are not careful."

Dalcour's brows raise, and I see the glint of his crimson eyes searching mine. Altrinion vampires have the ability to read most mortal minds, but I am not mortal. I can tell he's trying hard to read me. Unfortunately for him, his attempts will be like hitting a brick wall.

"Do not waste time trying to read my mind, vampire!" I shout, stopping him from ogling me further. "I am no mere mortal. If you want the truth, I'll tell you this: if even an ounce of that stone is damaged, I'll release the fires of hell where you stand."

"Monster!" Elysian shrieks, banging his cane against the floor.

As much as I want to keep Dalcour the target of my ire, I've grown tired of Elysian's waffling stance. Last night, I was his golden boy, all that stood between Lux and Winter. This morning, however, I am the monster. If he only knew just how monstrous I could truly be!

Tightening my jaw, I lock my fists at my side. It's all I can do to halt the fire burning my palms. "If you'd have me be the monster for the role I played in your son's disappearance, then so be it. Yes, Melchior was held captive in my care, but as I said last night, he was not my prisoner. While I may have seemed free to you, I can assure you, I was not. He and I were in shared captivity. If you want to look for a monster, look no further than the one at your side! Lord Marchand is hardly the prince of civility he'd lead you to believe."

"Trading insults, are we, Nyx?" Dalcour sneers, cackling as he claps his hands. "I'm pretty sure kidnapping someone and framing their death, all to trick his daughter into marriage, is quite a spell."

"What would you call the vulgar escapades of you and your kind over the years? The countless lives you've taken at your leisure, the blood baths held in brothels at your behest. How many mothers have lost sons and fathers their daughters? I know exactly who you are! When time comes for me to ferry your soul to hell, I'll be all too eager to ensure your voyage fits your revolting life."

Dalcour parts his lips to respond, but Elysian halts him, pressing his cane against Dalcour's broad chest.

"You dare spit out his monstrosities as though it should wipe clean your slate? I know not the mothers nor fathers that may or may not lament for Lord Marchand's supposed crimes. But I do know him. Never has he pretended to be anything more than he is. From the first day, I've always known who and what I was dealing with. But you, Kharon, I thought of you like a son. So much so, I literally offered my daughter to you—like a fool! You not only stole my son, you made a fool of me! For that, I will never forgive you!"

Watching the glassy pools gathering in the corners of Elysian's eyes hurts me more than he'll ever believe. This is not what I wanted.

Swallowing my pride, I lift a hand in surrender. "Please, Lord Elysian, I know there is probably no barter I could pay to make up for the ill I've caused you and your family. I can only hope that in time, you would come to forgive—no, understand my choices were not my own. Again, I implore you—do whatever you must to me —but please, I beg you, do not hurt the stone!"

"Ah-hem," Lux's brother calls from the corner as he and the woman continue holding Moirai's stone. "Lord Marchand, perhaps we should hear him out. I've never known one to lament over a stone. Surely, there must be more."

My heart smiles at his consideration. Looking at the woman I presume to be his mate at his side, the care in her eyes as she regards me is calming. Although it was Lux and his brother who stole my obol, I see more kindness behind his eyes than in Dalcour.

"Perhaps," Dalcour answers, rubbing his chin. "He could be bluffing. For all we know, he'll use the stone to thwart us."

Looking over my shoulder, a dark growl rumbles through me as Dalcour and I lock eyes. I've grown tired of his bullshit. Lifting my hands, I summon a gale of dark wind. The oak shutters on the windows shake and the cloth covering the transom blows, allowing fissures of light into the room. Lux's brother and his mate crowd into the darkest corner while the face of another less fortunate vampire is singed by the sun. The vampire releases a screeching cry, and Dalcour rushes toward me. I raise a palm in his direction, holding him back. Although I have no desire to kill anyone. I will. I'll kill them all.

"Nyx!" Lux's brother shouts from the corner. "Don't do this! Abigail and I will keep the stone safe!"

My eyes darken as the wind whips around the room. Dalcour's skin turns leathery red, his true vampiric face appearing. Small flames ignite from my palms; I have every intention of ending this. "Give me one reason!" I belt out.

"Because you love her!" Abigail yells across the room.

Abigail's words give me pause, and I look over my shoulder at her. With a trembling hand, she points to the door, and I see Rae, Ross and Stephen behind her, staring at me from the threshold.

Twenty-Seven

RAE

Nothing but darkness swirls around the room, and I can barely see anything or anyone, but I see Kharon.

He's bigger than he was this morning, his frame even more chiseled, with bulking biceps and skin that seems bronzed by fire. Seeing his flame-fueled palms aimed at Lord Marchand and my uncle sends a new fear rippling up my spine.

"Kharon, stop!" I shout, hopeful he can hear me amidst the whipping wind. "Please!" I plead once more.

Finally, looking past Marchand and Uncle El, Kharon sees me. His blazing eyes seem to burn a hole straight through my heart, hurt marring his perfect face. While I have no idea what happened before I arrived, I know Kharon is suffering. The look on his face is just as pained as it was when Lux kissed Win, breaking Melchior's curse.

Slowly, the dark wind subsides as the fire from Kharon's hands is snuffed out as he closes his fists.

"Rae." Kharon's voice is small, quiet, as if just saying my name were a balm to his soul. Cracking a dim smile, his eyes alone tell me he's more than happy to see me.

"Rae, shut the door!" Lux's brother, Cedric, shouts.

I don't move. I can't. I'm frozen, fearful that if I turn my attention in the slightest, Marchand will rush toward Kharon with whatever ill-will I see dancing behind his eyes. Thankfully, Stephen and Ross both rush to the door, slamming it shut behind me. A blessing, I'm sure, to the sun-scorched vampire at my feet.

"Pip," Ross whispers over my shoulder. "What in the hell did we walk in on?"

"Ross, Rae, you need to leave!" Uncle El barks, turning quick on his heel. I don't move. I will not. I need to know what's going on. My uncle plants himself in front of me and Ross, working hard to catch my eyes. He finally does, but I strain over his stout frame until my eyes once more lock with Kharon. "Stephen, please, get these two out of here!" he orders. Gulping, Stephen looks over at me and Ross before drawing his mouth into a thin line, refusing my uncle's demands. "This is not a request!"

"Khar," I quietly start, once more disregarding my uncle's pleas. "Baby, are you okay?"

Gasps erupt through my uncle's chamber, but I ignore them all. Kharon is all that matters now. While I indistinctly hear phrases of "I told you so" from Abigail and something about strumpets from Ross, it's only Kharon's words I need to hear.

Kharon smiles wide, this time reaching his eyes. I want to ask him what's with his transformation, but when I see his obol affixed at his jugular, I'm sure it's more Nether-magic I've yet to understand. Side stepping my uncle, I walk past him and Marchand, stepping over the injured vampire on the ground.

The wind lessens to nothing but a smoky breeze, leaving Kharon standing tall in the center of the room.

Walking up to him, my hands graze his chest, slowly trailing up to his chin. Taking his chin in my hand, I trail my fingertips through his golden strands, pushing a few tendrils behind his ear. Kharon runs his hands through my hair and kisses the top of my head.

"I'm okay, Rae," he whispers, as if we were the only two in the room. "Much better now," he adds with a kiss to my hand.

"How dare you!" Uncle El shouts, banging his cane into the floor. "It wasn't enough you imprisoned and nearly killed my son, then tried to entrap my daughter into a hellish union. Now you dare lay a hand on my niece?" Digging his cane into the ground, my uncle propels himself forward.

He rushes toward us, but Ross grabs his shoulder, holding him back. "Wait, Uncle. Before we jump to conclusions, perhaps we should hear from Rae." With a raised brow, Ross keeps a tight hold on our uncle, but his gaze remains cautious as he looks at us.

"Look, this is certainly not how I wanted to tell you—but here goes. Kharon and I love each other. We always have."

Shock and awe stir around us, but Kharon takes my hand in his. Once more kissing the back of my hand, Kharon looks around the room. Only finding a semblance of understanding in Cedric and Abigail, Kharon clears his throat. "Rae speaks the truth. Had you let me explain, you would know it was her love that brought about my physical transformation. While the kiss between Winter and Lux may have turned me into the grotesque thing you saw last night, it was Rae's kiss that broke the Changelings' curse from me. For that, I owe this beautiful woman my life."

"Hold on!" Ross yelps. With a wagging finger, he rears back. "You mean to tell me this is the one who you spend the night with?

Well, I'll be damned! Come on, Pip, you're better than this! This man was just pinning over Win yesterday." Ross doesn't give me a chance to reply. "My sister deserves better!"

"You're absolutely right! She deserves the best, and that's what I want to be for her. Not the Changelings' puppet, or a man who is forced to ensnare the kiss of Melchior's blood to not only free him but save the lives of my sister Moirai and myself from hellish servitude. That is the man Rae deserves and the man I'm trying to be."

"Ross, Uncle El, please understand. Kharon never meant to hurt us." Looking at Cedric and Abigail, I notice Moirai's stone, and now I understand the reasons for Kharon's rage. Pointing to the stone, I continue, "He's just trying to free his sister. Just like Melchior, she's trapped somehow in that stone. She needs our help. She needs her brother," I say, my eyes locking once more with Ross.

"I can hardly believe what I am hearing!" Uncle El snaps. I've never seen my uncle so furious. "Your mother is probably rolling in her grave at the woman you've become."

"And what of my mother, father?" The loud slamming of the door turns our attention. Seeing Melchior's pained face is more troubling than my uncle's words. "Is she rolling in her grave after all you've done? You're the reason the Changelings captured me, after all!"

Twenty-Eight

KHARON

"MELCHIOR!" Elysian balks at the sight of his son's glowering face. "Son, what are you doing here? Please, you shouldn't be here. The last thing we need to do is allow this, this *Ferryman* anywhere near you. I'd hate for him to imprison you again."

"He's right, Melchior," Dalcour says, coming to Elysian's side while keeping a pointed stare at me and Rae. "You really shouldn't be here."

"Oh, I know exactly where I belong!" Melchior bites back, brushing past Dalcour and his father.

Rae, Ross, and I share a look. We're all confused by Melchior's sudden outburst. Even Cedric and Abigail peer out from their dark corner as we trade puzzled glances.

"Whatever prison Nyx held me in was surely built by your hands!"

"Wait a minute, Melchior," Abigail interrupts in a syrupy soft tone. "What do you mean Lord Elysian is responsible for your capture? How is that possible?"

"Abigail is right," Dalcour interjects, his haughtiness again in full stride. "Changelings have no dealings with humans."

"Unless..." Cedric breaks into Dalcour's rant, stepping just beyond the shadows again.

"Of course!" I shriek as the puzzle pieces start to fall into place. "I always wondered why the Changelings were so intent on imprisoning Melchior. Surely he's not the first human to come across my obol over the centuries, but he is the only one they captured. The Changelings knew I'd be too focused on freeing my sister and myself from servitude to inquire further."

"Kharon, I don't understand," Rae says, tapping my arm. "Why would the Changelings want to hurt Melchior?"

"Elysian, tell me you didn't," Lord Marchand laments, pulling away from Rae's uncle. "Why didn't you come to me first? I would have told you—"

"You would've told me what? What could you say? Short of compelling away our desire to conceive our own child, what would you have me do? She wanted a child," Elysian counters. Turning to Melchior, he extends his hand. "She wanted you! Your mother would have traveled to hell and back to have you, son."

"So you used a Changeling Jinn?" I mutter in shock.

"Changeling jinns?" Ross questions. "Last night it was hybrids. I hate to think what's next."

Cedric steps forward, clearing his throat. "In the old days, people turned to Changeling jinns for fertility. Changelings trapped in Jinn jars would often trade their freedom for fertility.

The Jinn would possess the body of the infertile and live within her until she gave birth. In return, once the child was born, the Jinn would be freed. Once free, the Jinn could once again take form on this earthbound plane—a way of escape from the Netherworld. It wasn't normal practice for mortals, only supernaturals—"

Dalcour groans darkly, his crimson eyes glowing as he watches Elysian. "The Changeling Jinns are tricky. If they aren't freed as promised, they will reclaim the child, bringing a curse upon all those in the bloodline." Turning to Melchior, Dalcour continues. "Tell me, young one, before you found the obol, did you have dreams? Dreams showing you its location?"

"Yes," Melchior breathes back. His deep brown skin wrinkles in thick creases between his eyes. "The dreams were so vivid. Of all the rare treasures I found in dreams, the ones about the obol were clearest. I assumed I just had a knack for finding antiquities, but I never knew until—"

"Who told you?" Rae asks. "When did you figure it out?"

Looking over his shoulder, Melchior smiles. "Moirai." Both Rae and I share knowing glances, remembering how fondly my sister spoke of him. His soft smile fades as he turns back to Dalcour. "Moirai told me the Changeling used dreams to lure me to the obol. That's how they got me, and it's all because of you!" he shouts at Elysian.

"I guess now I know what else you're hiding in your vault. You've kept that Jinn jar all this time!" I reveal.

Dalcour's brown skin reddens once more. I almost fear his leathery, vampiric form will reappear, but staring at him, I see he's merely blushing mad. Good. I'd hate for Rae to see his monstrous form in full stride.

"All this time, you've allowed me to believe you were just an innocent bystander. It was all your fault." Dalcour's words lash out like a whip, but Rae's uncle holds his own, showing no sign of recoil.

"Would you have me sniveling and contrite before you, Lord Marchand? Is that what you think of us mere mortals? You come and you take and take! You say you're giving yourselves our protection, but you are not! Your balls and great halls all in the guise of civility, it's all a ruse! While I find no joy in agreeing with that hellion, one thing he said is right: the lot of you are monsters. So if I treated a monster poorly to get what I wanted, what was rightfully mine, what tear should I shed? I did what I had to do."

"At what cost, father? My mother died because you let that Jinn possess her!" Melchior breaks through his father's self-righteous admission. "Or what about my life? Does my life not matter? What about when I vanished? How could you stubbornly hold onto your sanctimonious stance?"

"Uncle El," Ross starts, making his way to his cousin's side. "Why didn't you say something?"

Turning back to Lord Elysian, Dalcour shares a brief look with me. I think we both know where this is going. "Oh, Elysian!" Almost whispering, Dalcour offers pained smile. "You could've come to me."

Tossing his hand over his head, he runs his palm against his balding scalp. "And say what? I've doomed my wife and child to hell? Who would believe me?"

I step forward. "Me." I raise my hand. "Maybe now is a good time to tell you a story about the Sons of Erebus."

Twenty-Nine

RAE

Everyone stands quietly, intently listening to Kharon share his life in the Netherworld, explaining how the Ferrymen came to be and how he's the first of his order to obtain an obol.

While Cedric suggested the Changelings were likely using both Winter and Melchior as payback for Uncle Elysian's refusal to release the jinn, Kharon believes Lux coming into Winter's life was a miscalculation on the Changelings' part.

"They never saw Lux coming," Kharon reveals, pacing the floor.

"How is that possible?" I ask. "If Moirai is a Fate at their leisure, isn't she obligated to tell them what she sees? You know, like an oracle?"

"Not quite. Fates only know the *what.* The *how* is always left to chance. She knows this is the course we had to take to secure our freedom, but everything in between is as much a surprise to her as it would be to anyone else," Kharon explains.

"So, this was always meant to be? *Us.* Like fate." I smile at the thought, taking Kharon's hand in mine, as if there was no one in the room but us.

"Like fate," he repeats in a whisper.

"Just wait one minute!" Ross clamors, clapping his hands to get our attention. "When Lux kissed Win, Melchior stepped out of a big block of ice. Are you trying to tell me your sister is trapped in that small little stone? What is she, a pixie or something? How could she possibly fit?"

"Moirai is—" Both Kharon and Melchior say her name in unison. Kharon's brow lifts, and it makes me wonder if something else is stirring between Melchior and Moirai than meets the eye. Extending his hand in surrender, Kharon gives way for Melchior to continue.

"Well, as I understand it, Moirai is trapped in her metaphysical essence in the stone. She lives out her physical form in the Netherworld. Binding a part of her consciousness to the stone allows her to speak with her brother in the earthbound realm."

"Okay," Ross drawls, pinching his chin as he circles our cousin. "I know I'm going to hate myself for asking this, but how does this Moirai speak with *you*?" Taking a long look at Melchior, Ross winks at me and Stephen, curiosity beaming in his eyes.

"All right, I'm not sure that's a proper discussion," Kharon protests, irritated as any sibling would be at the thought.

Melchior offers Kharon and Ross a crooked smile. "A gentleman never tells."

"A gentleman might not, but I'm burning to know," Ross whispers to Stephen.

Forcing a faux cough, Dalcour turns the attention back to him. "Well, now that we have a better understanding, I think we can agree you meant no harm. If the thoughts I've picked from your beloved's mind are any indication, I see there remains no malevolent intent. I owe you an apology." Extending his arm, he offers his hand to Kharon.

"Thank you," Kharon answers, shaking Dalcour's hand. "I want to offer my apologies as well." Turning away from Dalcour to my uncle, Kharon, curves his mouth into a thin smile. "Lord Elysian, Melchior, all, please accept my apology for the role I played. I promise, I'll endeavor to make myself worthy of your forgiveness, all of you," Kharon finishes, turning to me.

Melchior and Ross come to Kharon's side, patting his shoulders as my uncle remains still.

"If you think you can waltz in here and give me some backhanded condolences, you have another thing coming!" Uncle El shouts. "I will never forgive your betrayal of my family, nor will I ever condone this—this hellish union between you and my niece!"

"Lord Elysian!" Dalcour shouts, coming to Kharon's side before either of us can protest. "With the exception of the twins and their companion, no one in this room stands deserving of heaven, not even you. Sure, the lot of us may be monsters, but the role you played is not for nothing. It was your dealings that brought your family to this. You almost lost your son, and instead of being thankful for a second chance, you stand here, ungrateful and unrepentant!"

"Uncle El," I begin, tearful and heartbroken. "You say my mother is rolling in her grave at what I've become. What about what you are? Heartless. Mean. I've watched the loving and kind man I once admired turn into a cold-hearted fool!" A waterfall of tears race to my chin, and Kharon squeezes me at his side. I wipe my face before I start again. "I guess the good thing is, I was never looking for your permission. Sure, I'd like you to accept Kharon as you do Lux, but if not, so be it! I've lived in the shadows long enough, vying for your attention and acceptance. That time is over. No longer will I seek permission from you or anyone else for my happiness. I will be with Kharon whether you like it or not."

"Whether I like it or not, eh? Well, whether you like it or not, I consider you more than a niece. I see you as my daughter. Is it not enough that I have one daughter who'd rather live among wolves? Now you tell me you'd rather love this Ferryman. Why can't we find happiness with our own kind?"

Kharon grumbles, as does Dalcour, but it is my twin who steps forward.

"Own kind?" Ross begins, tilting his head with his eyes narrowed. "I can't believe my ears. I know this isn't the man who wrapped his arms around me when I was sixteen, assuring me that being gay was not some curse or something needing to be fixed. It was your acceptance that made my coming out story one of the easiest I ever told. You said only small-minded people loved small. You are the man who told me loving with a big heart was the only way to love. How can that be true for me but not for my sister?"

"Yes, and you loving Stephen, or any other man, any other human, is one thing. Stephen is not a monster! He's a human! That's all I want for my family: to love and to be loved. I just want them to share that love with humans, not wolves, or vampires, *or others.* Is that too much to ask?"

"Yes, Father, it is." Melchior circles Ross, stepping back into his father's line of sight. "So, it's okay to use a monster to make a human, but not okay for a human to use their heart to love a monster? Since I've returned, I've only seen one monster, and I'm standing here now, using whatever remains of my heart to love and forgive him."

Thirty

KHARON

This has gone on long enough. Seeing not only Rae but both Melchior and Ross heartbroken by Elysian is too much, and I can no longer remain quiet.

"A monster is only a monster if you give it power to be one. For some, a small spider appears as large as a dragon. While for others, a lion is nothing more than a big kitten. It's all in the eye of the beholder. Before yesterday, I was not a monster in your eyes. Until Melchior was set free, you saw me as a friend and advisor, someone you could trust and lean on."

"Yes, I did," Elysian admits quietly. "But for more than a

decade, you lied to me! How can I ever trust you, much less trust you with my niece?"

"Well, it would seem, my friend, we both told our fair share of lies. Whatever our reasons are, they no longer matter. All I ask is that you know the man you once trusted is still here. I've only ever wanted the best for you and your family. Nothing has changed."

Elysian grumbles incoherently. "But everything has changed! To learn all these years you've lusted after my young niece?"

My patience wears thin. "Firstly, Rae is a woman. I would never sully her reputation or treat her unbefitting of the treasure she is!" I roar back. "Second, last night was the first time we've ever been alone together."

"Ah-hem..." Ross snorts, cupping his mouth. Rae and I shared a puzzled stare before turning our attention to him. "That's not entirely true. I mean, there was that time on the ski lift a few years ago."

Rae giggles, bashfully turning away. Our faces blush and it dawns on me. I was right all along. Rae and I did share something special that day. She squeezes my hand and leans on my shoulder.

Elysian raises his thick brow as he rocks on his heel. Rubbing his chin, he eyes us both. "I don't know, Rae. I promised your parents I'd look after you two. That's all I ever wanted, but with both of my children intent on either chasing treasure or building schools, part of me always knew any legacy I'd leave behind would be better suited with you and Ross. I know Ross isn't taking those classes to pass the time," Elysian says, winking at his nephew.

For the first time, Ross is speechless as Stephen wraps his bulking arms around Ross' lanky frame.

"What about Rae?" Abigail chimes in from the side. Cedric softly shoves his mate's shoulder, but she smiles wide, throwing her thumb up and tossing a reassuring nod to Rae.

"Well, what about you, Rae? What do you want to do?" Elysian asks, smiling with tear-filled eyes.

Hunching her shoulders, she twists her small fingers through her hair. "Oh, I'm not sure."

"What about your bakery?" I suggest, kissing her forehead. She looks up at me, her eyes wide with surprise. "I'm sure that big recipe book of yours is full of delicious treats to add to the menu of the Elysian Manor B&B."

"Khar, how did you know? I—I, um—"

"Well, it's settled then! As long as my niece pursues her dreams of her own freewill, I suppose I can be a bit more tolerant and open to *what* or who she chooses to love." Elysian shifts a side-eye in my direction, but I don't care. Rae's happiness is all that matters.

Tossing her small arms around his round frame, she cries into his hold. "Oh, thank you, Uncle! Thank you!"

He pulls back some, wiping the tears from her face. "I am sorry for being such a cold-hearted fool. Your mother would be proud to see all you've become. *She is proud*. So am I!"

Rae and Elysian lock into an embrace, putting aside their differences. While instinct tells me there's more to repair between Elysian and me, I find comfort knowing whatever rift there was between them is slowly fading.

"What about Moirai?" Melchior breaks through the weepy reconciliation of his father and Rae. By the look in his eyes, I can tell he's not sold on the reunion. He and his father still have much to sort out.

"I have every intention of rescuing my sister," I reply, taking Melchior's shoulder in my palm. "Now that I have my obol, I can return to the Netherworld and free her once and for all."

"The time is not now, brother." Moirai's stone brightens in Cedric and Abigail's hold, and they both gasp in shock as a glow blasts through the room.

"What the fu—" Ross and Stephen shriek.

"Oh my word!" Elysian's eyes bulge as he stares at my sister's stone. He looks around the room, shaking his finger in bewilderment. "How—how is this possible?"

Letting out a hearty sigh, Dalcour removes his hat, revealing his thick curly mane. "In all my years, I've only glimpsed such power of the world beyond. This, I must say, is beyond me."

Finally, some humility from him, I think to myself. Rather than glory in Marchand's newfound humbleness, I turn my attention back to Moirai.

"Sister," I begin, kneeling as Cedric and Abigail lower the stone onto Elysian's table. "I have the obol. There's no need for you to endure the Changelings' torment."

"Yes, and you finally have a love to call your own. Take time to enjoy it." The light of Moirai's stone glows as she speaks.

"But what about you?" Melchior says, coming to my side. "When will we be together again?"

He keeps his attention on my sister's stone, but I can't help but smile as I look at him. Looking over my shoulder, even Dalcour, Cedric, and Abigail seem happy for Melchior. Thinking about how gooey-eyed Abigail and Cedric seemed last night, they are certainly one of those *"in love with love"* couples.

"When the time is right, my love," Moirai answers, and Melchior grazes the stone with his hand as though it were her hair. "Kharon," she continues, and I shift my attention back to her. "You will come to me when the first flower blooms. You and Rae will travel together to our realm."

"Rae?" Ross and Elysian yelp in unison. Shock rolls through us as all eyes turn to Rae.

Thirty-One

RAE

TAKING small steps between Kharon and Melchior, I stare like a deer in headlights into Moirai's stone. Allowing a momentary glance over my shoulder to Kharon, I hunch, surprised by his sister's instruction.

"Me?" My voice is small, but as quiet as it is now, I'm sure everyone heard me.

"Yes, Rae," Moirai answers as her light flickers. "This is how it was written, how it is meant to be. Fate has decreed it so."

"Fate my ass!" Ross protests. My uncle grumbles at his side, but it's Ross' daggered glare that cuts my heart in two. "There's no way

I'm letting my sister go off to some nether-place to save some invisible woman trapped in stone."

"Ross, please," I say, lifting my hand in caution. "Let's at least hear Moirai out."

"I've already heard enough. If these Changelings are powerful enough to bend Kharon and his sister to their will, what makes you think you can waltz your little ass in there without worry? Oh no! Absolutely not!" Folding his arms, Ross lifts his chin, narrowing his eyes as he watches me.

Uncle Elysian steps forward, but this time, he seems far calmer. Quickly casting a wary glance at Kharon and Moirai's stone, he takes my arm in his hand. "Rae, think about how they trapped your cousin. I couldn't bear it if they did the same or worse to you." A single tear falls to his round cheek, reviving my own waterworks.

Moirai's light flashes again. "I can assure you, Rae will not be in danger. She is not of Elysian blood."

"They're only after Elysian because he refused to free the jinn," Kharon adds. "I tested a strand of Rae's hair against their curse and it was as if they couldn't even see her. Winter, though—they recognized her."

"My word!" Uncle Elysian cries out and his face nearly pales at the thought.

Sauntering to the middle of the room, Dalcour lifts a hand. "If I know anything of the Changelings, they were betting on you uniting with Winter so they could ensnare her as well. They never had any intention of freeing you."

"Precisely," Moirai answers. "Rae is an anomaly."

"An anomaly they will never see coming," Cedric adds.

Grunting, Ross spins about the room, like we're missing something. "Um, am I the only person here concerned about my very mortal sister's ability to step into the Netherworld? I mean, will she be able to protect herself? She's not some supernatural being. This can't be safe."

"I will keep her safe!" Kharon declares. His tone is strong but not enough to be challenging. Supernatural or not, the look in Ross' eyes say he'd gladly go toe-to-toe with Kharon. I'm sure Kharon can sense Ross' trepidation because he relaxes his posture, gently palming my brother's shoulder. "Ross, if Fate has decreed Rae come to the Netherworld with me, it must be so. I promise you on my life, I will protect her with all that I am."

"Nyx," Uncle El interrupts him as he stands at Ross' side. "I don't doubt you'll do everything to protect my niece, but surely, you can make no assurances. If they were able to best you and your sister—"

Moirai's stone brightens once more, but this time, her light is nearly blinding. "My brother and I were not bested. We were given at birth to repay a debt we did not owe. Kharon is a Ferryman. He is empowered by the very stones the dead use as barter. Kharon, as you tarry to spring, you must locate the others. Every obol you collect strengthens your power to withstand the Changelings. You'll have the full power as a Son of Erebus. With Rae at your side, you'll have all you need to put an end to our imprisonment, once and for all."

Squeezing Kharon's hand, I look up at him and nod in affirmation. "Yes, Moirai. I will go with Kharon."

"I'll also go with you," Melchior rushes his words. "I can help."

"No, my love," Moirai replies. "I fear, should you come, the Changelings will do far worse to you. They've already cast a withering spell against you, speeding your age. If you come here, they will do far worse."

Ross and I look at each other, now understanding Melchior's pain while we skated.

"But—" Melchior protests.

Blaring light flashes through the room. “No, Melchior, for the Fates have decreed it so. Now, I must go.”

Taking her stone in his hand, Kharon’s eyes glass over, but he holds his sister’s stone tight. “At the first dawn of spring, dear sister, I shall see your face.”

Flashing brightly once more, Moirai’s light dims. Both Melchior and Kharon seem sad, but for different reasons. It’s clear Melchior is in love, and it is equally clear that Kharon loves his sister. I understand both men more than they know.

Turning to Ross and Uncle El, I offer a small smile, hopeful to ease their angst. Surprisingly, Uncle El seems keener on the notion than Ross, but my brother also knows me better than anyone in this room.

“Well, judging by the look in your eye, I know there’s nothing I can say to change your mind.” Begrudgingly, my brother twists his mouth into a smile as he opens his arms to me.

Throwing myself into his embrace, I squeeze him hard. “I’ll be safe Ross, I promise.”

Ross playfully pushes me away, like he does when he wants to stifle his tears. “You had better be, Pip. I’m serious, or I swear I’ll be the first gay man in the Netherworld, lighting it up like fireworks!”

Pulling me back to his side, Kharon laughs. “Pretty sure you wouldn’t be the first gay man in the Netherworld. Folks are rather fluid where I come from.”

Ross’s brows raise with surprise. “Ooh, well in that case, perhaps I should go. Hey, Stone Sister—"

Quickly tossing his bulking arm around Ross, Stephen gives my brother a stern look. “Oh, sweetheart, you’re not going anywhere.”

My brother smiles at Stephen, winking at me as my heart rejoices.

Thirty-Two

KHARON

SEEING the lovely smile spread across Rae's face is all I could ever want.

It seems like only moments ago, I had every intention of burning this place and everyone in it to the ground if any harm came to my sister's stone. Like all things Rae Vereen, though, she brought light where there once was darkness. Every desire I had to turn this place to ash quickly went away with just one look at her face.

That is why what I have to say is the last thing I want to do. Even more, I know it's certainly not what she wants to hear.

"Well, I can imagine Win's face when I tell her I'm going with you to the Netherworld. Talk about a shocker!" Rae shares a laugh with her brother. Ross buries his head into his palms, shaking it as they continue laughing.

"Oh, I'm pretty sure her pretty little curls will go bone straight the minute you mention Mr. Nyx," Ross snickers, playfully bumping his shoulder into Rae.

Dalcour sighs, shooting me a wary glance as he and Abigail care for the sunburned vampire. Tightening his mouth, his expression tells me he may know where this is going.

"Do you think it wise to tell my sister?" Melchior blurts, pulling my attention from Dalcour's glare.

Elysian turns to his son, trying to catch his gaze, but Melchior keeps his eyes on me, purposefully ignoring his father. "Ah-hem," he begins, patting his round belly as he steps forward. "My son has a point. Besides, Win just got Mel back. I sincerely doubt she'll be too thrilled to hear the news of *this—*" he motions his hands toward me and Rae, "*arrangement.*" While Elysian's tone may be dry and loaded with disdain, he's right about one thing.

Telling Winter about me and Rae, or the Netherworld, is not a good idea.

At her uncle's words, the glee-filled expression brightening Rae's face falls to a frown. "Uncle El, I know Win may not like the thought of me and Kharon, but she'll understand."

Cupping Rae's elbow, I shake my head in caution. "I don't know, baby. Your uncle and cousin may have a point."

Rae's wide eyes search mine, but she scrunches her mouth in such a cute, yet defiant way, it makes me want to take her in my arms and never let her go.

"It's not like it would be the first time Win heard how I feel about you. As a matter of fact, I told her as much just before the cotillion. All we have to do is help her understand you weren't responsible for Melchior's disappearance. Once she understands—"

Strengthening my hold on her arm, I give it a gentle squeeze. "It's not about her coming to terms with us, Rae. At least, not right now."

"Then what?" As she looks up at me through still wet lashes, it pains me more than she could ever know to say what I'm about to tell her. "What is this about, Kharon?"

"Remember when I told you that Fates can only give breadcrumbs?"

"Right, I remember. They can say the what, but not the how. So?"

Swallowing heavily, I exhale hard. This won't be easy. "Well, Moirai said you were an anomaly. It's important we keep you that way. We need to keep you off the Changelings' radar, especially if you are to go with me to my realm. Not only can the Changelings have no inkling of your connection to the Elysians, but we'll have to shield that part of you."

Rae's eyes fall but bounce back up to mine. "Shield how?"

"Remove your memories of us," Melchior chimes in. "They'll have to make it like we never existed."

"At least in your mind," Abigail whispers back. Looking at her, I am surprised to find tears behind her crimson eyes as she leans into Cedric's shoulder. "Only temporarily," she adds.

Throwing up her palms, Rae steps away from me. "Wait a minute! You're talking about erasing my mind. You can't be serious!"

Closing the distance between us, I move closer. I know she needs space, but I don't care. "No, beautiful, it's not what you think. What we're talking about is only temporary, as Abigail said."

"But why? How? I have so many questions," Rae grumbles, dropping her face into her hands. "Kharon, I can't lose my family. I just can't!"

Grabbing her wrists, I pull her hands away from her face, tipping her chin hup until our eyes meet. "I'd never let you lose your family, baby. Do you understand?" My eyes search Rae's and she grants a small nod, blinking hard to push her tears away.

"In this instance, Ms. Vereen, I'd think this is more about you protecting your family than losing them." Cedric's calming tone and generous smile is welcome. When he stole my obol, I swore I'd do everything in my power to end him and Lux. This morning, I couldn't be more thankful for his support.

Throwing an appreciative smile over my shoulder to both Cedric and Abigail, I look at Rae and smile. "Anything we do from here on out is to protect them. I promise."

The glint of hope from Rae as she gazes at me tests my resolve. She's putting every ounce of her trust in me by being here. The last thing I'd want to do is break that trust.

"Don't worry, Rae." Melchior steps beside us. "You don't have to do this right now. You have until spring before you need to take that step. I suggest creating some distance between you and Win, at least for a little while. That way, my sister won't grow curious, and your erasure should take better."

"We can help!" Abigail merrily adds. Before any of us can ask how, she rushes toward us, and Cedric halts her before she reaches the thread of sunlight peering through the shutters. Stepping back and grimacing at the sunlight, she shoots us an awkward grin. "Lux said he wanted Win to start school soon, so that should take up most of her schedule. He also wanted to take her traveling for a bit. Cedric and I can ensure they stay too busy to notice. That should buy you some space and time."

"Thank you," Elysian says. "Knowing Winter is kept far from this gives me comfort. I'd appreciate it if my wife is also not apprised of our dealings, at least for now."

Everyone nods in understanding except Melchior, who remains icy toward Elysian. Observing the tension between father and son, Dalcour's brow lifts.

"How did you know about this?" Dalcour asks Melchior. "For

a mortal, you are rather well-versed in all things supernatural." He folds his arms across his chest as he stares at him.

"Because it's what Moirai did for me. She erased my memories of my family. It was the only way to ensure the Changelings wouldn't know anything else about our family," Melchior explains. "Not until I was free of the curse did my memories come rushing back. It's been like an info dump. I'm remembering everything." Casting his father an ominous glare, I can tell there's more to Melchior's frustration than he's shared so far.

"But what about Win?" Ross questions. "You obviously remembered her."

Melchior's face darkens, and I can see remembering his torment is difficult, despite his strong and gallant demeanor. "Thoughts of little Win were the only thing I had to keep me sane. Memories of my last moments playing with her in the forest kept my wits about me for a while. That is, until Moirai told me how the Changelings were using my memories to gather intel about our family. Once she erased my mind, the Changelings had nowhere else to look. Since I came back, it's like everything hidden from me is flooding my mind. *Everything.*"

"That's why we can give them nothing, young one," Dalcour says, looking at Rae. "I can simply compel your memories from you," he offers with a cagey grin.

"No!" Both Elysian and I protest in unison. We share an understanding, albeit an awkward one.

Taking Rae's hand in mine, I try to force aside the eagerness of Dalcour's tone. I'm not an idiot. His lust-filled stare gives him away. Although I did it for my own pleasure, I think her snug ensemble may be accenting her curves more than I care for others to see. If he keeps it up, it will be the last thing his wretched vampiric eyes ever see.

"Look, Rae, I know all of this may feel like too much too soon. I won't ask you to do anything you're not comfortable with.

Decree of the Fates or not, I'll not risk your safety or ask you to give up your memories unless you are amenable. Only I will do it, no one else." I cut my eyes to Dalcour. Returning my attention to Rae, I smile. "It's like I said before, I'll never take more from you than I'm willing to give in return."

Despite the warring I see behind her eyes, she smiles. "I hope you plan to give me all of you, Kharon."

Damn. This woman is perfect.

Thirty-Three

RAE

Rushing back to the stables, I couldn't get away from my family fast enough.

Once we heard the jovial voices of Winter and Lux as they made their way back from the cabin, we abruptly ended our discussion. Being both Christmas and Winter's birthday, she'd quickly notice our disappearance had we continued.

After spending a better part of the day crooning holiday songs, drinking wassail, and lounging at the manor with the family, it felt like the minutes crept slowly as my heart ached to be with Kharon again. Sitting around a brood of couples made things more annoying, but at least I had Melchior to keep me company. Though he did his best to keep up his pretense, I could tell it pained him to be around Uncle El and away from Moirai.

Lord Marchand and Lux's family kept their distance from the manor. Although they're accustomed to being around mortals, they still prefer not to tempt themselves. Lux offhandedly joked we looked like walking meat sticks to them, and after some time, even the most subdued vampire can no longer fight their bloodlust. Thankfully, being a wolf hybrid gives Lux the advantage of not desiring blood, unlike his kin. I suppose being a wolf has benefits.

None of that matters to me, though. The entire time, all I could think about was Kharon. No sooner had all the happy couples commenced their swooning near the fireplace did Melchior and I take our rather unnoticeable exits. Well, I think I caught a quick glance from Ross while he and Stephen fed each other s'mores, but at least this time my brother knows exactly where I'm going.

My eyes scan the stables as I turn, about looking for Kharon. He assured me he'd be here waiting for me. Fidgeting with my fingers, I hover near Mr. Puddles. "Have you seen him?" I ask, running my hand through his slick mane. Only tilting his head slightly, clearly enjoying the gesture, Mr. Puddles only snorts in return. I wonder if he's answering me in some unknown language, as Kharon mentioned before.

"I'm right here." Kharon's voice startles me from the dark corner of the stable. "I told you I'd be waiting. I rather enjoyed stalking you all day, not that it was my first time." Kharon throws me a wickedly sexy smirk, and I almost want to ask him more. Instead, my mind drifts to times I felt like I was being watched, and I smile, knowing it was likely Kharon.

Smiling as Kharon steps forward, my heart nearly leaps out of my chest. I am so happy to see him. "So, what else did you do today?" I ask, trying to break away from the look he's giving me that will clearly have me naked in no time.

A few seconds of silence sit between us before Kharon decides to play along. "After taking Moirai's stone back to my place, I placed a barrier enchantment around the perimeter so no one can enter."

"You can do that?"

Kharon seems amused by the awe written across my face, but he shrugs his shoulders like it's no big deal. "Nether magic, remember? It's the same kind of magic I'll use to lock out the memory of your cousin before we go to my realm."

"Oh, is that why you didn't want Lord Marchand to just compel it from me? I mean, I know Altrinion vampires like him can do that."

Grunting, Kharon narrows his eyes as his palm squeezes my shoulder. "Firstly, I don't trust Marchand as far as I can throw him. Sure, we came to terms with the fact I was just as much a victim as Melchior, but that hardly makes us friends. If you haven't been able to tell, I'm not the overly trusting type."

Rolling my eyes, I scrunch my face. "No one knows that more than me."

Leaning his head to one side, his mouth curves into a soft frown. "But that didn't stop you, did it?"

Taking his chin in my hand, I shake my head. "You don't scare me, Kharon. I grew up around monsters, remember?" An appreciative smile spreads across his face, but he remains silent. "So, you're not friends. I get that. Tell me the second reason you didn't want Dalcour compelling my memory."

He shakes his head before answering me. "Vampires like Marchand would have most believe compelling is just some mindless control. On the contrary, it is a very intimate and intricate ability. The last thing I want is for there being intimacy shared between you. The only one sharing intimacy with you is me. Is that understood?" Kharon says with a firm hold at my back. He's got me pressed so tightly against him, I can feel the rigid steel of his manhood against my abdomen.

As much as I want for nothing than to lose myself in the moment, I know better than to do so here. Pushing back a bit, I try to change the subject. "I'm sorry to keep you waiting. I tried getting out of there as soon as I could."

Brushing his hair from his face, he dashes a sexy grin. "It's all right, beautiful. I would wait an eternity."

Kissing his cheek, I shake my head. "Liar," I say with a raised brow. He's not fooling me.

"Okay, you got me. Had you all sung that Bublé song one more time, I would've had stolen you out of there," he chuckles.

Poking his shoulder, I giggle. "Oh come on! You don't like *Let it Snow?* I mean, it's kind of apropos, don't you think?"

"Actually, I liked the Joni Mitchell song you sang while your aunt played the piano."

Twirling my fingers through my hair, I blush. "Oh, *River*. Yeah, I like that one too. It just felt different singing it this year."

"I bet." Kharon's voice seems to drop almost two octaves. Both the longing stare in his eyes and hardness of him against me as he pulls me close tells me all I need to know. "Let's go. I have something to show you."

Kharon doesn't give me a chance to respond as he quickly wraps me in his trench and sprinkles onyx sand at our feet. With one spin of his heel, we're invisible, flying through the night. This time, however, I take time to marvel at the faint shimmering lights illuminating the otherwise dark night.

A clear evening sky, nothing but the stars above us, twinkling Christmas lights below, it feels like a storybook setting. Who knew darkness could be so beautiful?

Landing near Kharon's cave, I'm surprised when he doesn't take us inside. Instead, he leads us to the side of his dwelling.

Removing his coat, we shimmer into view as Kharon takes my hand in his.

The sound of cascading water in the distance as we round the corner reveals a stately waterfall flowing into a large river. Rocks shine like glass as the water glides effortlessly over each stone as it makes its way down the brook. Not only am I surprised to see my first waterfall, but it's the sight of a long boat made from what appears to be bones and oak drawing my attention.

"Is this—" I gasp, covering my mouth.

A crooked smile curves at the corner of Kharon's mouth. "Yes."

Taking small steps forward, I lean over his ferry, looking inside. I'm surprised to find his craft sleek and smooth inside. "I thought there'd be more bones."

Hunching his shoulders, Kharon gives an almost bashful smile. "I could certainly add some if you think that's best."

Waving my hands in protest, I laugh. "Absolutely not!" Walking along the side of the boat, I reach out to touch it but pull back. "Can I?"

Gesturing his palm toward me, he smiles. "Of course."

"Okay, are you sure? I mean I'm not going to die right now or something?" I'm half serious.

Issuing me his smoldering, panty-dropping stare, Kharon dips his head low. "I can assure you, that is not your fate. If you'd allow me, I'd like to give you a tour."

A whiff of smoke blows by, and a dark cloud whips around me. In a flash, I look up to see Kharon now inside the ferry. Offering his hand to me, he pulls me up into the vessel in a smooth stride. The inside is bigger and deeper than it looks on the outside.

"Wow!" I shriek turning about. "How many people can you fit in here?"

"On occasion, I can get over two hundred souls on board." He says it so nonchalantly, I half expect him to burst into laughter. Instead, he just looks at me like he wants to devour me whole. I hope he does. "What do you think? Do you like it?" Kharon's voice sounds deeper, more lush than usual. I know he's trying to make small talk, but I feel like I'm missing something.

"Well, yeah, I guess," I shrug, fidgeting with my fingers.

"But?"

"I mean, it's just, this is where the dead go. Doesn't it feel kind of creepy to you?"

Laughing darkly, he saunters toward me. "Actually, it feels like home to me." Pausing, he takes my hand in his and catches my nervous gaze. "I want it to feel like home to you, too."

"You don't expect us to live here, do you?"

"No, of course not!" he laughs, palming his forehead. "Just think of it as visiting my place of employment."

We both laugh at the thought, smiling as we hold hands and look around. "Okay, I think I can do that."

"Hopefully, one day, it'll feel less creepy." Looking at me with another steely stare and giving me a sexy smirk, he rubs his chin. "Maybe I should add something that makes it feel warm and inviting?"

I grimace, clenching my teeth. "Pretty sure there's very little you can do to make this boat of the dead inviting."

"What about this?" he says, offering me a small rectangular blue box with a small red ribbon.

My eyes widen in surprise. "Kharon," I gasp. "What is this?"

"It is Christmas, isn't it? So... a gift." He smiles wide, his eyes dancing like a kid on Boxing Day.

"Oh, but I didn't get you anything. I'm sorry, I didn't have time."

"Just open it," he directs with a low voice.

Pulling at the ribbon, I slowly crack open the box in his hand. Moving a thin layer of tissue paper aside, the glimmer of a sterling silver frame shimmers in the darkness. It's the picture beneath the glass, however, that makes my heart thump wildly in my chest.

"Kharon—how? I didn't realize. You saved this? All this time?" My words must sound like a garbled mess, but I know he hears me. Looking at the picture of us, the sight of me nestled in his embrace warms my heart. I look so young, and he looks much older than he does now. Even still, knowing what I do now, all I see are two people desperate for each other.

"As soon as I got out of the ski lift, I grabbed the photo from the attendant desk. Everyone was busy with you, and the picture was just left there, so I took it. I've held onto it ever since."

Thick tears fall to my cheek at Kharon's admission. For years, I thought I was a fool to think someone like him could ever look past the confidence of my cousin, the whimsy of my twin, or even the control of my uncle to see me, the girl who stays hidden behind it all, hidden behind her own heart. I am no longer that girl. I am a woman, madly in love with the one who ferries my heart to new depths with every twinkle of his eye and kiss of his lips.

"Do you like it?" he asks with such an endearing stare, I want to be lost in the storm behind his eyes. A small nod is all I can muster. "Good. Now it's time for me to unwrap my gift."

Thirty-Four

KHARON

TUCKING her hair behind her ear, Rae's big hazel eyes look up at me, and every part of me is more thankful for the beautiful gift staring at me now.

"But Kharon, I wasn't able to get you anything."

Seeing the strong and stubborn stance she took before everyone today, I almost forgot the bashful, sweet woman I fell for resides in her.

"Oh beautiful, that's where you're wrong," I say, planting a small kiss on her forehead. She casts me a curious smile, biting her bottom lip. With just the look she's giving me, I know she knows where this is going. "You see," I begin, removing her coat. "I am a forward-thinking man. As such, I took the liberty of wrapping my gift this morning. Now, after waiting so patiently, I have the pleasure of unwrapping it."

Rae's mouth parts slowly and she shuts her eyes tight as I curve my hands along her body. The feel of her perfectly round ass, firm breasts, and cinched waist awakens a fire low in my gut. Thinking how I've grown since our last encounter, I almost wonder if her petite body can take me.

We'll cross that bridge when we get to it.

Squeezing my shoulder as she releases a small whimper, she whispers my name, biting her lip before opening her eyes. "It's so cold out. I'll freeze. Maybe we should go back to the cavern?"

"Do you trust me?" Dropping my hands to my sides, I await her reply. It's the longest five seconds in the world before she grants an approving nod, but it's the most worthwhile five seconds in my entire existence. "I want to take you on the ride of your life."

Tossing her head back, Rae's eyes close and her back arches, revealing her perfect bosom. With a wave of my hand, I chant the sacred words of the ferry, lifting the sails of my vessel, the boney foundation forming a ghastly skeleton crew at the helm. Rae's eyes pop open as she flinches, but I pull her to my chest, assuring her she is safe. She relaxes, leaning into my hold as I return my hands to her body. In one final tug, the fabric unravels from her body, falling beneath her like a cloud.

"Ignis Ardeat," I mutter, kindling the fire that controls my ship. Warm flames flare up at our sides, and Rae's eyes widen in surprise. "I'll always keep you warm, beautiful."

"Always," she whispers back as the ship slowly moves along the river.

Not able to wait any longer, I crush her lips to mine. Twisting and tangling our tongues together, the sweet taste of her mouth is a delicacy I can't get enough of.

Laying her down into the pillowy fabric below, having her flawless body laid before me now is truly paradise. The clanging sound of clashing bones against the rocky waters does little to dissuade the passion seeping from Rae's pores. Slowly parting her legs, I am once more in awe of the woman before me.

With one swipe of my hand against my body, my own garments fall to my feet, adding to our makeshift bed. My skin shimmers with the same fiery glow as before, but it's my enlarged size that catches Rae's attention as she gawks at me, taking in the full view as I grip my girth. Her eyes alone tell me of her uncertainty, but I know we can do this. *Together*.

"I know you can take it," I assure her, kissing her inner thigh. "Let me just prime you up a bit."

Instinct drives my tongue deep inside her center in one fluid motion. Adding my forefinger, I tap along her slick folds as I drink in all she has to offer. Her juices flood my beard, nourishing parts of me only Rae Vereen can. Lapping at her with an unquenchable need, I feel her pulsing along my tongue as my finger twists and turns until I feel her thighs tighten around my head.

"Khar!" she cries out, gripping my hair. "I can take you. Please..." Her voice trails off, but I know exactly what she needs.

I want to stay here, drinking from her until I'm satiated, but I'll not be greedy, at least not now. Since it *is* the season for giving, it's only fair I give my beloved what she wants. Pulling my lips from her sweet center, the sight of her writhing beneath me, glistening with her own arousal, practically pushes me into delirium.

Eager to be inside her, I thrust the first few inches in, relishing in her feral screams as her nails dig into my back. A part of me wants to ask if it hurts, if it's too much, but the yearning in her gaze gives me all the assurance I need to keep going. Rae grips my back, squeezing my butt, forcing me deeper.

Reaching between us, I run my finger along her plump, wet folds, spreading her; I need her to take the full width and breadth of me. *Every single inch*. I feel her tight grip loosen and I shove the remainder of my length inside. Rae screams, a high, lilting cry as her arousal drenches the fabric beneath us.

"Damn, baby, you're so fucking wet! My pretty pearl runs like a river!"

Shifting side to side, my hips keep rhythm with the rowing of the oars as they beat against the waves. I can hardly tell the sounds of Rae and the river apart. She feels and sounds *so* good.

Taking one of her breasts in my mouth, I flick my tongue against her nipple. She tightens around me as her sweet center pulsates along my length.

"Ahh... yes!" Rae whines as a gush of her nectar drenches me.

Just the feel of her vice grip along my length sends shudders up my spine, joy to my once withered heart. Driving deeper, I thrust in and out, side to side, quickening my motion until I feel myself come undone.

Filling her to the point of bursting, her name is all I can utter. As though we hadn't just gone at it like rabbits earlier, I'm still coming longer than I thought possible when Rae pulls me into a kiss.

This isn't a sweet, gentle kiss: this one is almost assaulting, owning me. With her petite fingers gripping the back of my neck, she holds me hostage, taming me with her tongue. Just the notion makes me come harder than I thought I was capable.

One lingering thrust and I smile into our kiss. "Ah... so you like giving me my gift, huh?" I lift up, gripping my still-rock-hard shaft as I admire this beautiful woman.

Rising to her knees, Rae's mouth drops open as she moans, turning her backside to me. "Not like. *Love*," she grunts, and my heart skips a beat. Licking her lips, she drags her eyes along the length of me, lingering just below my waist. "More," she moans, arching her back.

Well, I'll be damned: Rae Vereen has been kissed by fire, and I think she likes it.

Correction.

She loves it.

Next in the Fire Duet

Love. It's not something a Ferryman, a Prince of the Netherworld, ever hoped to attain. Yet, for Kharon Nyx, it's the one thing he is sure of. Rae Vereen loves him.

Despite his villainous past, her love kindled a fire deep in his soul.

But can she love him despite his present darkness?
As time is winding down to save his sister from the Netherworld, Kharon and Rae's love will be put to the test in ways neither of them thought imaginable.

With dark secrets revealed, the fragility of their world will expose whether their love can truly endure.
Will the darkness of his world douse their kindling flame? Or will their love burn brighter than before?

Preorder** Fire Born **now!

More from L.C. Son

Explore the books and short stories of the Beautiful Nightmare Universe:

Books

Beautiful Nightmare (Book One)

Hearts Eclipsed, A Beautiful Nightmare Novella

Awaken: Beautiful Nightmare (Book Two)

Untamed: A Beautiful Nightmare Story

Beta Rising

One Winter's Kiss: A Beautiful Nightmare Story

Fire Kissed & Fire Born Duet (Netherworld Series Debut)

Coming Soon

Breaking Curses: A Beautiful Nightmare Novella

Broken Moon

Beautifully Dark Things- Planned 2024

Dawn of Descent: Beautiful Nightmare (Book Three) TBA

Short Stories

I AM NO WITCH: A Beautiful Nightmare Short Story

With Clipped Wings of Butterflies: A Beautiful Nightmare Short Story

With Hearts Like Fire: A Beautiful Nightmare Short Story

For more info on my books, visit:

My Books & Short Stories - L. C. Son Books (lcsonbooks.com)

Remember leaving reviews makes you an MVP!!

About L.C. Son

Known for her Amazon Best Selling Short Story, *With Hearts Like Fire*, and the series starter, and epic fantasy novel, *Beautiful Nightmare (Book One)*, L.C. Son is the happy wife of more than twenty years to her high school sweetheart and a loving mom of three.

Growing up, she spent hours reading comic books she "borrowed" from her older brother, which inspired her love of heroes and all things fantasy and paranormal.

Much like the characters she adored, she lives a duplicitous life. By day, she works tirelessly to champion the employment of persons with severe disabilities. By night, she puts on her wife-mom cape, sharing with her husband at their church and juggling their kids' highly active schedules.

Presently, she's working on the next installment in the Beautiful Nightmare series.

For the latest info and to join the member-only newsletter, visit: www.lcsonbooks.com.

CPSIA information can be obtained
at www.ICGtesting.com
Printed in the USA
BVHW041945060423
661903BV00004B/146